SOMETHING BEAUTIFUL

The Blisswood Brothers Book 4

EVEY LYON

THE BLISSWOOD BROTHERS

Something Right

Something More

Something Good

Something Beautiful

ABOUT

Drew doesn't believe he deserves to have something so beautiful, and falling for Lucy Blisswood would be reckless anyways...

The worst thing a guy can do is fall for your best friend's little sister, so imagine when all three of her overprotective brothers are your friends. It's a simple rule to follow: don't look at Lucy the way she looks at me. And when she returns to our small town of Bluetop unplanned, keeping her off-limits should be the least I can do. After all, the Blisswood brothers made me an honorary member of the family, they gave me a chance when nobody else would. Which is all the more reason I can never admit that I wish I didn't have to stay away from Lucy and her persistence.

And in a moment of weakness, I don't.

But Lucy understands me like no other, and we both share wounds and secrets—including what's transpiring between us. Soon we find ourselves finally confronting what feels like a romance years in the making. I know it's a betrayal to her brothers, and I definitely won't get points for what I do with her when she's wearing only my shirt. Not to mention, Lucy deserves Bluetop royalty, not me. But when I get life-changing news, Lucy's determined not to let go. She makes me feel special, and I know that I shouldn't push her away. Because I think I'm finally discovering that what Lucy and I have… makes me feel that I may finally be worthy of something beautiful…

This unrequited love, brother's-best-friend romance is the fourth and final standalone book in the small town Blisswood Brothers series that follows the brothers as they run their family winery and farm, Olive Owl.

DREW

I don't know why I bother eying the menu as if I need to make a choice. I always order the same thing, without fail—chicken salad sandwich with a side of fried pickles. Nonetheless, I skim the menu on the wall before placing my request with the new recruit behind the register at Sally-Anne's. I even order a chocolate malt since it's Saturday, my cheat day, and it's freaking hot outside.

Stepping out of the way, I take a spot on the spare seat along the windowsill. I'm not sure why this place isn't busier today, but I guess it's 3pm, so not quite lunch or dinner time. This place is a Bluetop staple, mostly breakfast or early lunch, though. You can't go wrong with what you order here... except the coffee, that's just for if you have a death wish.

My phone vibrates in my pocket, and I pull it out to see that I have a message from Grayson.

Grayson: Hey, Drew! Throwing steaks on the grill tonight. Come join us.

Normally, I would say yes, but I want an easy night in tonight, maybe practice a few new songs on my guitar. It's been a busy week, as Grayson and I have been working on a new house one town over. Well, he designs, and I handle the construction crew. In fact, Grayson is so embedded in my life that he's more than a friend, a boss, a mentor... he's my brother. We may not be tied by blood, but he and the Blisswoods are the closest thing to family I've ever had.

My thumbs tap along the screen.

Me: Thanks, but I'm doing a late lunch and need to catch up on sleep.

Grayson: Okay, but feel free to swing by tomorrow. Pool and BBQ.

I pause for a second, knowing he won't relent. Then the corner of my mouth tugs.

Me: For sure. Tell me what to bring.

Grayson: Nothing. Well, that is until it's tomorrow afternoon and I realize that I forgot to pick something up at the grocery store and need you to save my ass.

The sentence finishes with a winking emoji.

Me: Truth.

I send a peace sign.

Grayson is a true family man; he'd do anything for his kids and wife. He has two daughters, with another child on the way. They all have him wrapped around their fingers too. He also makes good business decisions, as proven by the fact he started Blisswood Homes since he leaves the running of Olive Owl to his brothers. Olive Owl is the other place where I spend my days, as I still help Knox and Bennett with the winery, the place I worked at for a few years.

Speaking of which, my phone rings, with Knox's name flashing on the screen.

"Hey, man, everything okay?" I greet him because I know he went to Chicago for the day.

"All good, but I kind of need a favor." I can hear the smile in Knox's voice. He is the Blisswood brother closest to my age, the youngest of the three brothers, and my boxing and drinking buddy too.

I chuckle, because when Knox asks for a favor, it can be normal or out-of-this-world random. "Go on."

"Madison and I decided to spend the night in Chicago for a little getaway, you know how it goes." I can only imagine, but I don't *know*. I've had girlfriends, but nothing that made me see a future with any one of them. I know I'm capable of envisioning it, I have, just not with them. "It's a bit spontaneous, which means we didn't make arrangements for Pretzel." Ah yes, their monster-sized dog who captures even non-dog-lovers' hearts.

"Need me to go check on him?" I ask as I tip my head in thanks to the server who hands me my bag of food and drink.

"Exactly. He needs his dinner and a trip outside. Maybe in the morning you need to swing by too, or you can just take him home with you and we will pick him up tomorrow," Knox explains, and I can hear the sound of a crosswalk signal in the background.

Taking a quick sip of my chocolate shake through the straw, I assure him, "No probs. I'll take him home with me."

"I owe you."

"Sure. Next time at Rooster Sin can all be on you." I smirk as I exit the café and the little bell over the door chimes. Knox and I go to the bar a couple times a month, I even sometimes perform a few sets on my guitar there, so it's an easy compromise.

Hanging up, I balance my food in one hand as I throw my sunglasses back on. Looking around Main Street, I notice it really is quiet this weekend. I guess a lot of people are out of town, a phenomenon I never quite understood, as Illinois summers can get mighty warm. We aren't in the suburbs of

Chicago, but we have plenty of nature around. Then again, I guess palm trees and clear blue water are more appealing.

Opening the door to my truck, I slide in and turn the key so I can listen to some music. I'll quickly eat my fried pickles because those are best eaten warm. A sound of excitement escapes from me when I see they added an extra side of ranch dressing to dip them in—a classic combo.

I'm proud of my truck—the latest model, bought with my own money. I've worked hard for this, along with my small two-bedroom house that I renovated with my own hands. I would never have imagined this as an eighteen-year-old, but now I'm twenty-four and have my shit together.

Donovan Woods's "Clean Slate" begins to play on my speakers. I'm always on the lookout for songs with good acoustic strums.

My phone lights up again, and I roll my eyes when I see the incoming text from Kimmy, a hook-up from months ago. *Want to hang out tonight?*

That's a solid no. I have zero interest, so I type back that I'm busy and to take care, hoping she gets the hint that it's a long-term *take care with your future endeavors that I don't need to know* kind of thing.

My eyes land on the white envelope in the side pocket of the passenger seat door. It's been sitting there all week, taunting me. But I'm not ready to address the contents of the letter quite yet, and I'm quick to ignore it again.

After finishing my pickles, I start my journey to Olive Owl. I admire the small town that I grew up in, a simple place, yet somehow it has this sophistication that marks us as what some would call "quaint" on any tourist map or blog.

In truth, I should have left when I finished high school. I had no reason to stay. My mom disappeared when I was a kid, and my dad—or Keith as I call him—we had an odd relationship, more roommates than anything, so I wasn't surprised he left when I hit my eighteenth birthday and he was no longer responsible for a child.

I was at a loss for what to do at first. Join the military, finish high school, start working—I was officially clueless.

Until the Blisswood family came into my life.

They gave me a job, Grayson paid for my community college courses, and they welcomed me into their family.

Arriving at Olive Owl, I still appreciate the beauty of this place. It's chic, with well-manicured landscape around the farmhouse that is modern yet has classic detailing. It's both a home to Knox and a few rooms upstairs for the bed-and-breakfast. Normally, there are guests if they come for a wine tasting, but not this weekend.

I put in the code for the security system by the back door and immediately I hear the sound of big paws padding against the kitchen floor. I open the door a crack, and sure enough, I'm greeted by a giant ball of white, brown, and black fur. A Bernese mountain dog that is Knox and Madison's child.

"Hey, buddy." I pat his head and try to calm his excitement, as one little hop with his paws brings him nearly up to my shoulders. Pretzel whimpers a sound. "I know. Want to go outside for a bit?"

As I open the door, he runs out and directly to a bed of flowers to sniff.

I shake my head, amused, before grabbing an extra can of dog food and a bowl to take home with me, plus his leash. Then I decide that since I'm here, I'll check on the wine barrels in the barn and the sprinkler system for the fields, as we aren't expecting rain for a few days. Even though I know Bennett—the middle Blisswood brother—has it always under control, he's also been busy with his two kids.

It must be forty-five minutes later when I return to the

back patio to look for Pretzel. Calling out his name, I get no answer. I'm not worried, though; he normally has the run of the place and always returns.

Still, I head down the stone path through the garden and down by the willow tree. It's next to the pond, and when I see Pretzel sitting at attention with his tail wagging, I notice he's staring at something—or rather someone.

I follow his line of sight to land on the woman swimming in the pond. The water is clean enough, but not always warm. Either way, I'm not sure anyone really swims here except Knox and Madison when they get a little wild, skinny-dipping and all—I walked in on that once. Quickly, I scan back to the bank and notice the pile of clothes on the big rock where the water is ankle-deep.

Squinting so my sight can focus, I survey the person who is swimming. But my heart already began to thrum a few seconds ago, so loud that the sound buzzes in my ears.

My body already feels the answer.

The woman swimming is no stranger. She isn't even trespassing. This is her land too.

She must have noticed I'm watching, as she swims back to shallow water.

Swallowing, I try to get a grip on this unexpected surprise.

To everyone else, Lucy and I are friends. For the most part, that is true. Except sometimes you have an unspoken connection with someone, and it haunts you some days because the bond runs so deep.

But as she emerges from the water, the sun is nearly blinding me, causing me to see only the outline of her mostly naked body—a perfect hourglass curve, her long legs disappearing into her skimpy underwear, her bra well filled, and her tits perky. Yes, my mind notices, because she is no longer a teenager. She's twenty-one, still snarky and frustratingly persistent.

Water droplets drip down her body. Her long hair is darker than before, and the smirk playing on her lips is admittedly tantalizing.

"Drew," she says my name, and I fight hard to stay composed.

"Lucy," I answer, and my eyes stay fixed on her, as if I am a man possessed and someone would have to pull me away to stop this locked gaze that I have on her.

She takes a moment to assess me from head to toe before she grabs hold of her hair to wring out the water. When she pulls it up over her head, it causes her chest to push out, and her entire body arches into a posture from any man's fantasy.

Ten seconds in and she is already taunting me.

"I didn't know you were back." I try to stay on track and remain fucking unaffected.

Her hair falls as she grabs her clothes. "It's a surprise. I texted Grayson only a half-hour ago. I needed to clear my head, so I thought I would come here. I'm back for the summer."

Fuck. She could say an hour and that would be too long. But a whole summer?

A thought in the back of my mind has me feeling suspicious that something isn't right. Ever since Lucy went off to college, she's never came back for the full summer only little breaks. With one year to go until graduation, I'm not sure why she feels the need to end that tradition now.

She flashes me a sly smirk, before turning so her back faces me. I bring my closed fist to my mouth to bite the moment she unclasps her bra and throws it to the side.

Looking to the sky, I pray for a miracle to end this scene.

Lucy pulls her dry t-shirt over her body, which doesn't

fucking help, as it's white cotton. She glances over her shoulder, giving me a warning grimace, and that's my cue to look away.

Shaking my head, I turn around and look down at Pretzel whose head is cocked to the side—lucky bastard, he gets to watch.

Soaking-wet black panties land on the grass by my feet which indicates that Lucy took them off.

Hell is looking like a good option right now; I'm already being tortured.

Lucy clears her throat to give me the all-clear. I pivot slowly back around to find her now in jean shorts, which means she has nothing on underneath—not helpful.

Her hands find her back pockets as she stands there.

For a thick few seconds, we stare at one another. Jesus, why does she get more beautiful every time I see her? And that's not the worst part. Why does she have to be the one who saved me in ways she will never understand?

Friends are what we should be.

She deserves to be with Bluetop royalty, someone from a good family, who will give her a great life with all the creature comforts she grew up with—horse included.

But her look is enough to make me want to offer her the world if I could.

Except I won't.

Because Lucy has three older brothers who I owe my life to, and the last thing they would ever want is for me to lay a finger on their younger sister.

And if they knew what thoughts run wild in my head, then I would already be a dead man.

Life has thrown me hardships, but I would live them all over again if it would mean, in another life, I could have a chance with Lucy Blisswood.

But we only live one life, with my current situation being the one I got.

And I have to figure out a way to cope.

Because Lucy just stepped closer to me, her tongue darting to the corner of her mouth, and her look is a promise that I won't be able to walk away.

2

LUCY

Drew's deep blue eyes pierce me, and I notice how his lips close together, as if he's trying to keep in the abundance of frustration that I know I cause him. His nostrils enlarge to the point his dimple forms, and it only confirms my theory.

But I won't touch him. I've learned my lesson once, and I'm no longer a teenage girl with a crush. Over the years, I've come to value that our friendship, if that's what we can call it, is worth more. Doesn't mean he leaves my thoughts or that I don't want to test the waters.

"What are you doing back, Lucy?" His voice has an edge, and his question has a hint of concern.

I glance down at my brother's dog who is drooling up a storm from the heat. "I just… wanted to see everyone—"

He cuts right in. "Bullshit. Why are you *really* back?"

The corner of my mouth curves up, because already he sees through me.

Drew is older than me; when I was a freshman in high school, he was a senior. Often absent from school, he stuck around to get his diploma then stayed in Bluetop. In truth, unless you hate small-town living, then there is no reason to escape Bluetop, as it's tranquil and quaint. The people are good here.

Drew never left, partly my brothers' doing. In my mind, I remember being sixteen, when Drew ordered me to get in his truck because he could tell that I was upset and didn't want me to be alone. It was after school, and on the drive to my house, I tried to hide a tear. Grayson had just moved back to be my guardian after our father's death, and guilt filled my lungs, because I'm not sure he would have come back otherwise. When I asked Drew why he felt compelled to drive me home, he answered so simply, *"Because you have beautiful tears."*

When Grayson saw me in Drew's car, he assumed the worst, but that was short-lived. Shortly after, Grayson invited Drew into our world, and to my dismay, that made Drew even more of a fantasy that I could never have.

Remembering that he asked me a question, I comb a strand of wet hair behind my ear. "I need a break from college life, okay?" I begin to walk away, as I know he will only pry more.

Of course, he stalks behind me. "It's summer. You're on a break, so why do you make it sound like it's more than that?"

I pick up my pace as I walk toward the main part of Olive Owl.

"Lucy," he nearly barks out. It's so frustrating that this man cares too much.

He won't relent until he knows the truth, and like I'm a pile of rope twisted and knotted on the floor, he will be the one to undo it all.

"Just let it go," I say in an attempt to steer him away from his investigation.

Pretzel runs ahead of me onto the patio, yet I feel Drew's presence behind me, and it's overbearing.

"Never in the last three years have you just shown up out of the blue, so why now?" Drew treats me like a sister sometimes, but I know the moment I turn around that it will confirm that he sees me as anything but.

And like a woman who wants to be punished, I pivot to look, with all my zero resolve for this man evaporating.

"I'm dropping out of college." The sentence fumbles out of my mouth, and the moment I realize what I admitted, I feel the dread as Drew shakes his head side to side in disappointment.

A long silence takes over as he studies me, and I look at the ground with a sullen feeling.

As a teenager, I was the smart girl, the high achiever, the one who persevered through everything life threw at her. I pushed on when my father died when I was sixteen and watched as my brothers found their new families. Even when Knox fell for my favorite teacher, I took the situation like a champ. I've been the most perfect princess that anyone could ask for.

Truthfully, college was something I thought I wanted. Majoring in English and living somewhere new seemed like a great idea. For the past three years, I've called upstate New York my home, with days filled with classes and summers occupied with extra courses.

But I've made a mistake somewhere along the line, and sometimes you just need comfort in the familiar.

My eyes draw a line up from the ground, running along the outline of Drew's body, jeans with a dark hue that only highlights his blue eyes more, and a dark t-shirt that makes no sense in this heat. His arms are crossed over his chest, yet I still manage to see the tattoo of an arrow on his inner arm. I know he's contemplating what to say.

"Does Grayson know?" It's a simple question.

"No, nobody does. And I would appreciate it if you kept this between us until I tell my brothers." The pure disdain for what I will have to do drowns my words.

Drew reaches out to touch my arm. "Lucy, is everything okay?"

Damn it, that sincerity is back again.

"It's fine. Can we just talk about this another day?" I plead, and I try to avoid my eyes landing on him.

"Okay."

My head perks up in surprise that he's agreeing. "Really?" I ask in doubt.

He nods, his lips quirking out. "Our secret. But I'm going to tell you that you're making a mistake. Plus, the moment I think we need to worry, then it's game over and I tell Grayson."

I throw my hands up in aggravation. "Fine. You know, your loyalty to Grayson is a real pain in my ass." I begin to walk away again, this time with big, long strides in the direction of the barn.

"Lucy, I don't need to explain why." He follows me with a quick pace as I abruptly open the barn door. "What are you doing, Lucy?"

I throw him a glare over my shoulder. "Seeing the horse, since everyone replaced Cosmo so easily."

Growing up, I had a horse named Cosmo. He was a gift when I was six, because having three older brothers and a father meant I was sometimes spoiled. My mother died when she gave birth to me, so the men in my family did their best to raise me. Especially, as there is a nine-to-fourteen-year age difference between me and my brothers. And I do appreciate the life they gave me, which is all the more reason why I fear the discussion ahead when I break the news.

My eyes land on the Cosmo replica chewing on some hay. He's a large brown horse with a dark mane.

Hearing Drew snicker, I turn my head to look at him, and for the first time, I see a smile forming on his mouth, clearly amused. "Jealous?" he asks.

"Why would I be jealous of the horse?" My hands find my hips.

Cosmo was old, so when Knox phoned me before Thanksgiving my sophomore year of college to tell me to come home, as they were going to put Cosmo to sleep so he didn't live in pain, I understood. I cried a lot, and for one brief moment, I remember whose arms I cried in… he's standing in front of me.

But why? Why did they replace Cosmo so easily? I know it's a ridiculous thought, it's just…

"*Astro* is fine. I gave him water earlier," Drew informs me as he watches me.

"I know Rosie got to name the horse, but really? Why not just name the stallion Cosmo 2.0?" I snap then walk to the horse to stroke his fur, because it isn't his fault that he was gifted to my niece because Grayson has no spine when it comes to his daughter. Nor is it Astro's fault that Rosie wanted to rhyme with Cosmo. I mean, I guess it's kind of cute, and he is a gorgeous horse.

"Rosie is eight, give the kid a break," Drew reminds me.

"I know," I nearly sulk. "Just strange being back and feeling like everyone has moved on," I admit.

Drew steps forward to join me in petting Astro. "That's how life works, Lucy." He lets a loud breath escape. "You're going to stay at Grayson's?"

"I guess." I shrug. "I mean, I'm sure Knox and Madison

would let me stay here, but I feel like they may need space, enjoy their newlywed life and all."

He scoffs a laugh. "They've been married a while now."

I give him a knowing look. "Knox also mentioned baby-making during a recent video call, so I'm going to take a pass on the chance of witnessing any of their efforts."

Drew's grin is suave. He has boyish looks, yet his grin always reminds you that he's a man. A strong man who has been through things, yet he still manages to smile like it makes the world turn.

"And Bennett?" he suggests.

We both laugh. "I am in no way walking into a life with two boys under the age of five." Raising a shoulder to my ear, I succumb to the easiest solution. "Grayson has such a big house that I can escape if needed, plus I have my old room there. The girls are there, and with Brooke pregnant again, then maybe I can help them out."

Grayson built his house my senior year of high school after we'd lived in the house my father moved me to a few years prior. I'm the reason Grayson left his fancy architecture job in Chicago, and when he came back to Bluetop, he was forced to take responsibility of me until I turned eighteen. He didn't seem to mind, even less so when he realized his now-wife was our next-door neighbor. And even though his guardianship of me would come to an end at age eighteen, he insisted on having a room for me to return to on college breaks.

Drew nods in approval. "I'm sure they would like that, with helping out, I mean." A smirk plays on his mouth that makes my heart skip an extra beat, especially as he raises a brow. "Since he has a pool, then why did you come to Olive Owl to swim in the pond?"

"To clear my head before the family ambush." And it's

the literal truth. Olive Owl belongs to my family, and I'm a Blisswood, but I make no mistake that it belongs more to my brothers than me. Olive Owl is their passion and business; to me it's memories of childhood and only that. "I know Knox is in Chicago, but I wasn't expecting *you*."

He laughs. "Sorry. It was a last-minute request from Knox. I'm taking Pretzel home with me for the night."

I look at my fingers drawing a circle on the neck of the horse. "Oh. Just assumed you would be going to Rooster Sin or have a date," I pry as casually as possible.

His eyes narrow for a second, as if he knows what I just did. "No, I mean, not tonight. There isn't… anyone." It sounded like he struggled with informing me of that fact; he even glances away.

"Right." I give Astro one last pat before indicating with my head that Drew should follow me out.

After closing up, and Drew calling Pretzel to his car, we find ourselves next to his shiny new truck. A far cry from the beat-up one he drove when we were teenagers.

"Wow, an upgrade." I touch the silver paint on the door of his car.

Drew weaves his hand through his hair. "Yeah, got it a few months ago. It makes sense, as I need to move a lot of wood and supplies for the construction work, plus sometimes Knox needs me to help out at Olive Owl." He looks around and then it dawns on him that my Prius is here. "You drove all the way from New York?"

I tilt my head to the side. "It isn't as far as you would think, if you go via Michigan."

He whistles a sort of hiss, a hint that he's on to me. "You're not joking about the break, are you? You don't drive from New York, unplanned, with your car and all, unless you want to move."

"Don't start. Not you," I warn him.

He holds his hands up in surrender. "I'll say no more."

"A man of few words. Surprising," I retort with sarcasm. "Even when your face tells me you're remembering certain things."

"Be happy I don't bring it up, otherwise it could get aw —" He stops his sentence when he realizes what he was going to say.

Rolling my eyes, I fold my arms over my chest. "Thanks. I was trying to avoid reminding us of…" I wave him off. "You know what, I'm outta here. I guess I'll see you around."

As I storm off, I hear him call my name. "Lucy, I'm sorry, it just came out."

I close my eyes, and my fists form at my sides. My back is to him, but he must also know what's going through my mind with that reminder.

I was eighteen and decided it was my chance to offer myself to Drew. I figured he was holding off on touching me until I was a legal adult. I was so naïve. With a bra that accentuated my breasts under a tank that exposed enough to make his eyes wander, and shorts that barely covered my ass, I showed up at his place after dinner one night.

The moment Drew opens the door, his eyes survey my body from head to toe. Admittedly, although hungry-looking, he seems to grasp right away the reason why I'm standing before him, ready to offer myself.

"Lucy," he grits out a warning.

I step closer to him, determined, as if I can edge my way into his house, but he stops me with his hand gently pressing against my shoulder. "I think we should talk," I say. "Now that I'm legal and off to college, then there is nothing in the way stopping us—" Confident words flood out of my red-

covered lips, but Drew stops me by placing his warm hand on my cheek.

"Don't." His voice is sharp, but then it softens. "Don't do this."

Our eyes meet and lock, the air growing tense between us. "It's you that I wa—"

He continues to shake his head, indicating for me to stop speaking. A sour feeling grows in my stomach because I don't feel like he plans on kissing me.

"Do you ever think about it?" I ask him in reference to us.

His lip twitches slightly in response. No words come out of his mouth. Instead, he leans down and gently kisses my cheek. "Go home," he whispers, and I swear I can hear the pain in his voice.

"Why?" I hear my voice crack, even in a soft low tone.

"So many reasons, but I would rather you stay in my life, and this is the only way." He pulls back, with his thumb stroking my cheek one last time before leaving me standing there on the front stoop.

The memory fades out of my head, the reminder of his vow that I hate. I turn around mid-parking area and hold my hands out at my sides. "You know what? There is one thing that nearly stopped me from coming back. Want to know what it was?"

Drew looks to the sky then back at me, suddenly mute.

"It's you." The biggest headache in my life. He has the ability to shape my heart or break it. He lingers in my mind as a constant *what if.* I could scream and he would come running, but only if it was to save me and nothing more.

"I'm not going anywhere, so why did you come?" he asks simply, and I notice his breath picking up by the movement of his chest.

I choke on words as I debate what to say. "Because I'm lost right now… and I hate to admit it, but you are my fucking compass."

Turning, tears sting my eyes as I get into my car and slam the door. He doesn't chase me, and I knew he wouldn't.

Instead, he watches me drive off, because watching me is the one thing he is a master at.

3

LUCY

Looking at the bedside clock, I see it's almost ten in the morning.

After last night at Olive Owl, I drove around, picked up some take-out food from the new fast-food place near the highway, and quickly met up with an old friend. By the time I made it to Grayson's house, everyone was asleep for the night. Even Grayson who'd been waiting up for me was asleep on the sofa with the television on; he must have dozed off.

Rolling out of bed, I grab a fresh t-shirt and throw it on. With an elastic band around my wrist, I pull my new shade of dark hair up into a ponytail. I dyed it only the other week, a reddish-brown.

I look at my laptop on the desk, and although I know it's Sunday, I head to my keyboard, input the password, and hit refresh on my inbox screen that is always open. Of course, no new emails. I've been anxiously waiting weeks for a possible solution for my road ahead, it would only take one email... Alas, nothing.

Blowing out a breath, I know it's time to head into the

chaos for the day. At least breakfast smells good; the aroma of frying bacon is what woke me.

As I leave my room and head down the stairs, I can already hear dishes moving in the kitchen and the sound of little kids playing with toys.

One deep breath and my feet land at the bottom of the stairs on the smooth floor, then I walk straight to the large kitchen. The entire house is open-plan, with high ceilings, and every detail was designed with perfection and a lightness.

"Auntie Lucy!" Rosie squeals and runs straight to me, still in her princess-themed pajamas. I quickly catch her for a big hug.

"Hey, Rosie!"

"Daddy says you're going to stay with us."

"Sure am." I set her back down and look up to see Brooke smiling at me over the stove where she's cooking something, spatula in hand. Her light brown hair is still long, and she looks radiant in a summer dress shaped around her body, her pregnant bump peeking out on her slender body. Her raised brows also inform me that she knows there must be a story coming.

Brooke sets the utensil down and circles around the kitchen island. "Lucy, it's good to have you here. And your hair! It's darker." Her arms come out to give me a warm hug.

"It was time for a change," I answer simply in her embrace.

Pulling back, she studies me and rubs warmth into my arms. "You okay?" she mouths.

I nod yes.

The squeal of a two-year-old breaks my attention, and I see my niece Bella wobbling as she pushes one of those little carts filled with blocks. There are a few tiny teeth on display with her giant smile.

Leaning down, I coo a greeting that gets me a giggle before I stand and head to the kitchen island.

"Coffee?" Brooke asks as she busies herself in the kitchen again.

"Sure."

"I'll get it," Rosie offers, heading straight to the coffee machine, and I look between Rosie and Brooke, confused.

Brooke proudly smiles. "We have her trained."

I smile at her answer. "Where's my brother?" I ask curiously.

It causes Brooke to smirk. "Went for a run before I put him to work. Family BBQ today, in case someone forgot to give you that memo."

Internally I curse to myself, but I throw on a fake smile. "Oh, joy."

Rosie brings me my coffee for which I thank her, then I take a sip of the decent brew.

"Auntie Lucy, do you have a boyfriend?" Rosie heads straight to the hard questions as she climbs up on a stool to sit at the counter.

"No boyfriend," I answer plainly and focus on my coffee.

"Guy from your study group didn't work out?" Brooke asks innocently as she places bacon on the paper-towel-lined plate.

Tucking a few strands of hair behind my ear, I swallow. "Uhm, nope. Total bust." A partial truth. I shake off all thoughts and refocus our attention. "How is the pregnancy?" I take the plate from her to set it next to the buffet of breakfast food she has created on the counter.

"Easy. Maybe third time's the charm, or maybe I'm too busy with the girls to even notice that I'm harboring another one due in September." Brooke seems absolutely happy as she holds a mug of tea in her hands, swooshing the tea bag around.

"Still no clue if it's a boy or girl?"

Rosie pipes up with a piece of French toast in her mouth. "It's a surprise. Daddy says either way he is outnumbered by princesses."

"Daddy also thinks Mommy barefoot and pregnant in the kitchen is the way life should always be," my brother announces from the direction of the hallway to the garage.

His voice brings a blip of excitement to my body, purely because I enjoy seeing my brothers after time away. I didn't come home at Easter, and Christmas was a quick two-day trip.

Grayson looks the same, with piercing eyes, well-trained physique, and a little stubble on his chin. He smiles at me and brings his arms out to indicate he wants a hug.

My palm flies up. "No way. You're sweating like a pig."

He chuckles and gives up, instead walks straight to Brooke to kiss her cheek and rub her belly.

Maybe I was wrong and staying at Olive Owl is the better option. Brooke and Grayson are one of those love stories that will always make you feel like you're witnessing the reality of a romantic holiday card. They were each other's first loves, reunited later in life, and they own it.

Grayson snatches a piece of bacon and chomps a piece off. "Listen, I love that you're back, but an unplanned visit is very unlike you. You are an organized over-planner. Everything good?"

I offer him a wry smile and lie. "Totally."

His eyes survey me for a moment, but he doesn't press. "Okay, Lucy. Well, stay as long as you want. I just thought you have extra classes this summer."

I answer maybe a little too quickly because I've rehearsed this. "I can do them online."

He doesn't seem to question that. "Okay." A wide smile forms on his face. "We can count on you for a few nights of babysitting?"

Laughing, I feel like I'm sixteen again. I was Rosie's babysitter before Grayson and Brooke found their way to one another. "For sure."

"Hey, I don't need a babysitter," Rosie protests, and all the adults look at one another.

"But Lucy can help you with Astro," Brooke mentions.

"Yep, Cosmo 2.0 and I may become great friends," I say dryly.

Rosie perks her head up. "He's *my* horse."

My eyes bug out, and I point a thumb in her direction as I look at her parents. "Someone developed an attitude."

Brooke and Grayson smile awkwardly. "A work in progress," Brooke promises.

We all make our way to the dining table, and Grayson touches my arm to pause me. "Good to have you home."

"Thanks."

Home. But is it my heart or just my body that's here?

———

BREAKFAST WAS A LAIDBACK AFFAIR, with focus on the kids and what's on the menu for the BBQ. Of course, Grayson realized that he forgot a few items on the list that Brooke gave him yesterday. Her stern look of disapproval was erased the moment I offered to head to the store.

At the supermarket, I used the time to wander through aisles, when in reality all I needed was a bag of nuts for the salad and a block of cheese. Debating cracker options was purely a tactic to buy time, because I knew the moment I returned back to the house that the whole tribe would be waiting.

Walking around the house, with the sounds of splashes in the pool and men laughing, I brace myself for the Blisswood interrogation. The smell of grilled meat feels like a saving grace, as it always tends to mellow my brothers out.

The moment that I turn the corner and Grayson tips his head up to indicate for my brothers to look, everyone, the dog included, looks at me.

A communal, "Hey," drums in my ears.

Before I even get a chance to set the bag of groceries down, I have Bennett hugging me, with his toddler Joel in his arms. He only has to step away a moment before Kelsey, his wife, engulfs me into a hug.

"Your hair is gorgeous!" Of course, that's the first thing she would say since she owns a salon.

"Thanks. Where's J.J.?" I look around and see my five-year-old nephew is occupied swimming with Drew holding him in the pool.

It's a family affair, so yep, that means Drew is here.

"How's my favorite student?" A bikini-clad Madison comes to hug me, with her sunglasses on top of her head to keep her blonde hair out of her face.

"How's my favorite teacher?" I return in the same sing-song tone.

Knox cuts in and scooches his wife away. "Of course she is rocking, she married me."

I shake my head ruefully before he bear-hugs me.

Silence except for the sizzling of the grill overtakes the air, and I realize everyone is looking between me and Drew.

"Aren't you two going to say hi?" Knox raises with confusion.

"We ran into each other already yesterday," Drew mentions as his eyes return to safe-keeping my energetic nephew from drowning.

"At the gas station, by chance." Why I don't want them to know I went swimming at Olive Owl, I don't know.

But nothing I say in the next half-hour will make sense.

Bennett hands me a beer bottle. "Here, have a drink since you're legal now."

It causes me to smirk, because true, I haven't had a lot of chances to drink within the law and my brothers be present.

Luckily, Brooke and Kelsey are eager to get snacks, and Grayson is focused on flipping burgers. It's another scorching day, and I dressed with my orange bikini on under my clothes, so I quickly whip off my shirt and shorts, throwing them onto the lounge chair. My eyes can't help but wander to see if Drew flinches, and I do catch him quickly looking away.

"Auntie Lucy, will you play mermaid with me?" Rosie runs to me and quickly pulls my arm. My niece gives me the perfect opportunity to enter the water and taunt the man who still makes my chest flutter. Sweetly smiling at my niece, I follow. "Of course."

Walking down the steps into the pool, the cool water hits me, but it's refreshing. I make a point to stay in Drew's vicinity who is catching my nephew who keeps jumping in, only to climb out and repeat the process.

Drew has definitely been working out, as his chest is more defined, and I now notice his arrow tattoo on his arm in more detail. Making a point, I ensure to splash him as I dive under the water.

My niece is already collecting colored sticks on the bottom of the pool, and I join her before we emerge again. It doesn't take long for her attention to move to another activity, which is lying on her unicorn floaty.

Stepping through the shallow water, I lean against the side of the pool.

"Burger or chicken breast?" Grayson calls out to me.

"Chicken, please," I reply as I turn in the water and rest my head on the deck and let my legs float.

"Don't forget my veggie burger," Rosie calls out from her relaxation on her unicorn.

Grayson salutes her. "Of course, completely prepared for vegetarian-experiment week two for Rosie." He looks at me and shakes his head. "Rosie decided she wants to be like two kids in her class."

I nod in impressed approval.

Knox comes to sit down next to me, beer in hand, and his feet land in the water as Bennett follows suit, with Grayson looking on at my two shirtless brothers.

Crap. The time is upon us.

"So, why the unexpected arrival, Lucy? Is there some guy we need to hunt down?" Knox asks as he drinks a sip from his bottle.

I'm not even going to feed his curiosity, mostly because anger is boiling within me. Instead, I cop out with fake concern. "Aren't you happy to see me?" I wiggle my fingers against the edge of the pool.

Bennett and Knox both have sunglasses on, but they somehow give me a knowing look. "Of course we are." Bennett dips his hand down to splash water at me.

I fall back into the water to create distance. Floating on my back, I'm still facing them.

"This is unlike you, that's all. Don't you have summer classes?" Bennett leans back to rest against his arms.

"I can take them virtually."

"You're, what, just going to hang around Bluetop for the summer?" Knox tips his head slightly to the side. "What about your apartment?"

Glancing at the water, I avoid their gaze. "I sublet it to a friend for the summer." Another lie, because I gave up the apartment altogether, but the landlord still needs to handle the paperwork.

Bennett shrugs a shoulder. "That makes sense. I guess with your last year coming up, you want to kind of have a calming summer. Not sure if being around us is relaxing, but maybe I get it."

His theory is something I run with. "Exactly. Anyway, I guess I can help occasionally with my nieces and nephews. I'm useless at Olive Owl but sign me up if you're desperate."

Grayson shakes his head. "Between us men, I think we have it covered. Besides, you should focus on school, and you'll be back to college in August anyhow," he says over the sound of searing meat.

My head turns in Drew's direction who is now sitting on a step in the pool. His look is tight, with the gentlest shade of disapproval.

"Right." My T is sharp. "Back to school in August," I repeat Grayson's words.

For a moment, we all look between one another, unsure if this is the end of the conversation. I'm sure my brothers have theories, or they are dying to press for more answers. But one thing that I've learned over the years is that having a large family means discussion is easily interrupted.

Point proven by Brooke returning from the kitchen with a big bowl of salad in one hand and Bella resting against her hip in the other arm. "Almost ready? Trying to figure out nap times for this afternoon," Brooke inquires, oblivious to the interaction happening in front of her.

"For sure. Alright, troop, we are ready." Grayson dishes burgers onto a plate.

Bennett rubs his hands together as he moves to stand. "I'm starving."

Knox is still looking at me, his sunglasses now tipped down on his nose so his eyes can assess me. He's always been the brother to offer me an out. But maybe he is who I would let down the most. Because he always warned me that I may burn out if I didn't slow down. Or is it Grayson and Bennett that would be flooded with disappointment? They were always so excited for my overachieving ways. It could also be my father, who left me a trust fund for college. Basically, every man with the name Blisswood won't be happy with me.

And as I swim to the steps, I'm greeted by a steely look on Drew's face.

"Really going to lie about this?" His tone is low and nearly a growl.

"Yes. Now if you'll excuse me, I have a chicken breast calling my name." I march up the steps.

Because he isn't spared from being on the list of people who will look at me differently when they find out the truth.

4

DREW

A coffee at 3pm is probably not a great idea. I always try to cut back on my caffeine intake after lunch, otherwise I have trouble sleeping. But it doesn't matter anymore, because the last week I've had trouble sleeping anyways, and the few days since I discovered Lucy is back, then I've slept even less.

I'm sitting in Bear Brew, Bluetop's local coffee spot. The owners try to set a hip vibe, with a bear drawing on the wall, but really, as the only place in Bluetop with specialty coffee, then they don't need to do much to attract people. Unless you ask Sally-Anne at her café and bakery, because she never got the memo that she is not a contender for best coffee in town.

Sitting at a table along the window, I stare down at the envelope that's been screaming at me for days. I've read the letter maybe twenty times, and although clear, my thoughts are not. I have a decision to make, and curiosity to fulfill, but it may just be for the best that I ignore the letter for a little longer.

Since there's only me and one other person sitting at Bear

Brew, I notice right away when the door opens. My eyes instantly snap up to land on Lucy.

Great, exactly what I need right now. And that's not true, either.

I can't deny that, in our strange way, we talk with one another from an angle of pure understanding. Nor can I deny that the image of her in a bikini is now imprinted in my mind, and I'm fighting my guy to stay down in my pants.

Lucy brings her sunglasses to rest on her head. Her hair is down, and the more I see it, the more the new color suits her, and her sea-blue eyes are now bolder. She has on a loose tank, shorts, and sandals, with a tote bag on her shoulder. The smirk on her face greets me and also indicates that she is pleased by this surprise.

Quickly she orders something at the counter then slowly walks to my table to flop right in front of me on a chair.

"What brings you here on a weekday afternoon?" Lucy questions as she gets comfortable on the chair.

"Needed a coffee, and I'm done for the day. We started the construction crew at the ass-crack of dawn to avoid the afternoon heat." She nods as if she accepts my reply. "What are *you* doing here?"

"Brooke dropped me off while she does errands, and I'm going to try and work a little." She pats her tote bag with a random pineapple on it.

Lines form on my forehead. "On what? More lies?" Her mouth gapes open at my words, clearly offended. Instantly, I feel like an ass. "I'm sorry, that shouldn't have come out like that."

"What should it have come out like?" That sass in her tone is a downfall of mine. It weakens me because her snark is inappropriately hot.

The barista arrives with an iced coffee for Lucy, and that

would have been the right menu option to choose for a summer day. Instead, I already finished a traditional black coffee with no bells and whistles.

Lucy sips from her straw as she stares at me and waits for me to speak. Her arms are folded over her body for effect.

"Well, you buried yourself in lies at the barbecue. For one, they think you're taking summer courses…" I hold up my index finger. "…Are subletting your apartment." Another finger comes up. "…And three, returning to college for your *final* year. Your last year, which means you're almost there, so why give up?"

She stares at my three fingers in the air before rolling her eyes to the side. "I know, okay." She doesn't seem thrilled with those facts either. "I just need a little more time."

Leaning back in my chair, I want to keep pressing her on this because she is capable of so much and I don't want her to throw it all away.

"What are you running from?"

"Please," she pleads faintly. "Can't we talk about the things we used to? Like ridiculous things?"

A smile tugs on my mouth because simple conversation with her is also a comfort. "Okay." Her face softens. "Have you seen the menu at the new fast-food place?"

Her expression turns to relief, and her eyes and grin come blazing out. "Yes! Oh my gosh, I nearly died when I saw they have a fried onion covered in cheese, ranch dressing, pickles, and your choice of bacon bits or *pineapple*."

"I bet it's good, though."

"Yeah, because you have an obsession with ranch dressing."

I grin. "It's God's holy work."

Her cheeks tighten and the line of her shoulders relaxes.

"And I also saw that Rooster Sin now has two nights where buffalo wings are two-for-one."

I scoff a laugh. "That's right, you're legal now, so you can finally go."

"Yep. I'm going with Kendall one night this week." She stirs the ice in the cup with the straw.

"She's around?" I inquire about her best friend from high school. The former cheerleader is a complete opposite to Lucy.

"Only for a week, as she has an internship starting. So I guess it's me and the fam for the rest of the summer."

Now I need to grin at her forced enthusiasm. "They love you," I remind her.

"I know. Can I share a secret?" she humorously requests and scoots closer to the table as if someone is trying to overhear.

"Always," I say, playing along, but it's the ultimate truth.

"My niece has turned into an absolute princess that needs to be reined in." She fakes a disapproving look.

I laugh. "Well, I know you're not talking about sweet Bella, so that means the only culprit is Rosie who, yeah, I've noticed is a little… bossy." But I'm not going to highlight that fact with Grayson, I don't have the guts to.

An easy calm comes over us as we smile at one another.

"Still helping Coach Dingle at the high school?" Lucy moves her drink to the side.

"Oh, you know it. He has me and every Blisswood brother roped into helping with whatever sports season it is. Football training starts in early August, and Grayson has already been recruited. But I only help occasionally."

"And boxing with Knox?"

I slowly nod my head, as her brother is my boxing partner. "Sometimes twice a week."

Her eyes flick up from the table. "And guitar?"

Maybe she saved that question for last because she knows how much joy I get out of it.

"Almost every day. Actually, I'm performing at Rooster Sin this week."

A sly seductive look forms on her face as her fingers play with a napkin. "Is that an invite?"

I chuckle softly under my breath. "It's a public place, you don't need an invite."

Her mouth quirks side to side, and I'm not sure when she notices but her eyes lock on the envelope that has been lying on the table. "What's that?"

My heart feels heavy, yet my body numb, if possible. Or maybe it's because I've turned off all feelings in relation to it.

"Just… something I… Life takes turns, you know?" I now seem to be talking to myself as I swallow.

Lucy's demeanor instantly changes, and now she grows concerned. "What happened?" Her body straightens and all her attention is on me. "Is it…?" She doesn't want to say it.

She means my parents. My mom left when I was six, and my dad wasn't much of one.

"Let's forget about it."

"You have a secret too," she mentions simply because we both have something we're hiding.

Blowing out a breath, I lean over the table and slide the envelope to the side. "A secret for a secret? You share yours and I'll share mine?"

Lucy's eyes squint as a wry smile forms. "I'm onto your scheme."

"Well, if you change your mind then you know where to find me." I begin to get up.

"Will you let me in this time?" Her question is playful,

and I know she means my house, because our attraction is always simmering beneath us.

I shake my head. "Not even going to answer that." She should know better. "I'll see you around."

"Yeah, Rooster Sin, because you invited me." Now she's teasing me.

"Bye, Lucy." I can hear the smile in my voice.

Walking out of Bear Brew, I head to my truck in the parking lot behind the building and off Main Street.

When I reach my car and I'm about to open the door, I hear Lucy calling out my name. I look up to see her walking at a fast pace with her bag hanging off one shoulder and my envelope in her hand. My body instantly panics.

"Hey, you forgot this." She stops in front of me.

Quickly, I snatch the envelope back. "Did you read this?" My tone is harsh as I examine the paper.

Her face indicates that I need to settle down. "No, of course not. It looks private. But now you have me scared. Should I be worried?" She rebalances her weight between her feet to stand tall, as if she needs to show me she can handle it.

"It doesn't matter," I snap.

"Bullshit. What has you acting like an asshole?" she challenges, with her eyes never blinking.

Opening my car door, I throw the envelope in. "Forget it, Lucy."

As I'm about to slide onto my seat, I stop in my tracks when I hear her speak.

"I'll tell you." Her tone sounds like she is surprising herself with her admission. Looking to her, I can see she is desperate for information. "An exchange. I'll share if you share."

I scoff a sound in doubt.

Leaning against my truck, I cross my arms over my chest

and study Lucy. It's in that moment that I realize she may be bursting to share because she doesn't take any joy at all from keeping everything inside.

"It's not an even trade, trust me." She has no clue what's coming, because neither did I.

She cocks her head slightly to the side. "Want to bet?"

"No, I don't," I answer mundanely and look at the ground. The sun is beating down on us, and it doesn't help ease the stakes of admission.

"On spring break, I got involved with my professor's assistant." The shame in her voice is clear.

When my eyes snap up to look at Lucy, I see her gaze is in the far-off distance. Inside me rage builds, for so many reasons. That she shouldn't let some asshole be the reason she's leaving college is one thing. But at this moment, the idea of another man touching her is excruciating.

When Lucy went to prom her senior year of high school, I purposely didn't show up at her brother's house until after I knew she had left because I didn't want to see her in a dress on the chance that I would feel something. And throughout college, when Lucy has dated, I've somehow muted my ears when her family would discuss it.

Because deep down I know that I wish I could claim her as my own. It's an infuriating fantasy that I do my best to bury.

The news she just shared is pretty much the shovel to unearth every notion in my body when it comes to her. For that reason, I feel my blood boiling, and I'm uneasy.

"Lucy," I begin. I'm not sure I have it in me to hear any more details. Instead, anger erupts within me. "You're back because of some guy? Of all the reasons in the world that could have you upset, it's that?"

Her mouth parts open and her face flushes red. "Smooth.

The guy of few words is quick to judge me. You know what, why did I even bother? It's not like you're going to try and understand or even level with me as to why you are in a mood in general."

She begins to walk away in a huff. In a split second, I try to figure out what has me upset—her news or the fact I've been lost for weeks.

I don't want her to walk away. Quickly, my mouth opens and I say the words that I have yet to say aloud, but I want her to stay. "It's my dad. The envelope, I mean... apparently my real dad."

My plan does the trick, because Lucy stops and slowly turns back to me with her face now in shock. "Real dad?"

"Yep." I rub my hand over the back of my neck. "The good ole' biological kind that you never knew about since you thought some other asshole was your father."

It takes a few seconds for it to register with her. The fact that my dad who didn't do a great job of parenting wasn't my dad at all. Instead, there is another man in the world who I have yet to meet that shares my blood.

Immediately, Lucy runs to me and wraps her arms around me. The warm hug is a pleasant surprise, the kind only she could give. I inhale her grape scent, and I note how her body feels. It's an innocent hug, but it's enough for me to imagine what it would be like if she were closer, and harder pressed against my body.

Lucy pulls back with a gentle calming smile. "Want to go get fried onions with the works or maybe just a bowl of ranch dressing?"

Because our revelations call for a longer talk.

5

DREW

God, this feels like a throwback.

After Lucy texted Brooke that she has a ride back later, she hopped up into the passenger's side of my truck as if it were a daily occurrence. We didn't say much except for the occasional mention of something new in Bluetop. The whole time, I couldn't help taking side glances to get a glimpse of Lucy in my car.

It was a warm spring day when I offered a sixteen-year-old Lucy a ride home in my beat-up truck. She was upset, thought Grayson was mad at her. She was moody because Lucy has always had a snarky streak, and not in a vicious way, more entertaining than anything, and it makes everyone smile. But it was our start. We would hang out, drive around, say nothing or say everything. I never gave any indication that it was more, even when she turned the magical number eighteen. I somehow remained a respectable man, even if it was a struggle.

Except the looks we shared over the years was already enough, because maybe in another life, we would have had a chance.

And here we are now, parked in a field, with our feet dangling as we sit in the back of my truck eating fast food.

Lucy pops another curly fry into her mouth. "This was a good decision. I can think clearly now." Her focus on her food, along with her sounds of satisfaction, are distracting.

"Oh yeah? Going back to college?" I prod as I rip off a piece of fried onion.

Her response is to throw a fry at me. "Is now the moment we head into a deep convo? Because I think you get the award for who has the bigger life-changing event."

Sipping from my drink straw, I tilt my head to the side in contemplation. "But is it, though?"

Lucy looks at me like I'm crazy. "Um… yes."

Setting my drink to the side, I sigh.

"Start from the beginning." Her tone has so much care and patience in it.

"What? How I found out about my father?" She shrugs. "You know, I always wondered why Keith never really felt like a dad-dad, you know?"

She flashes me a humorous understanding look. "Well, you did call him Keith, so yeah, there was an indication that something was up."

I like how she's making this light, not heavy, and I need that.

"I mean, my mom left when I was young, said being a mother wasn't what she wanted. And Keith, well, he was okay some days, but it was no loss when he left when I was eighteen either. I guess I assumed being a father for life wasn't what he wanted. I mean, he literally said, 'You're eighteen now, an adult. I did what I had to do, and luckily you don't need me anymore. Take care.' His obligation was over. Now it makes sense."

Lucy slides the food a few inches to the side then scoots

closer to me. "Even if it makes sense, it still sucks that it happened."

I shrug a shoulder. "It's the hand I was dealt, and many people turn out just fine without parents. At least I got one partial one."

Her lips twitch at that thought. "So how did you find out about your real dad?"

A long breath draws out of me as I lean back and prop my arms up. "A few months ago, I got a letter from a lawyer saying his client believes that I might be his son. My mom was only sixteen when I was born, and he was too and had no idea. It was a one-time thing, he wasn't even from her town. Apparently, one of my mom's old friends from high school was dying from cancer and had a long list of secrets she felt she needed to tell, and him fathering a child was one of them."

Lucy touches my arm to pause me, as she seems to be taking in my words. "Really? Wow, this is kind of crazy."

"Tell me about it." I look down at her hand. It's on me. A gentle feathery touch that ignites something in this instant —comfort.

"Okay, so he didn't know either. That's maybe a good-bad thing. Bad that he didn't know, good because it means he didn't abandon you on purpose. Is abandon perhaps a shitty word to use? Oh man, I know I majored in English, but this situation calls for incorrect grammar and word choices," she mumbles, and she looks all around and seems almost embarrassed, thinking she is making this conversation uncomfortable.

"Incorrect grammar and word choices sound like a good plan," I assure her. Her eyes refocus on me, satisfied with my answer. "Anyways, he had a private investigator find me, his lawyer asked for a paternity test, I did it out of morbid curiosity, we got the results, story is true, and now he wants to meet me," I explain in one long slew of words.

Lucy's mouth cracks into a half-smile. "Okay, that's the speedy version of events, but I shall accept it. The letter?"

"Hudson, that's his name. Hudson Arrows. He wrote me a letter asking for us to meet and shared his contact information. His lawyer already did that, but he felt he should try a different approach because he doesn't want to show up out of the blue."

Lucy straightens her shoulders. "Hudson and his lawyer. Sounds like this guy is kind of fancy."

I snicker a sound, because now I'm entertained.

"What? I mean, it costs a lot of money to do all of that. He really wanted to find you."

Scratching my cheek, I prepare for the shriek that I know will escape her mouth. "Probably because he has a lot of money. He coaches some big NFL team."

"What?!" she shrieks. "As in football?" I slowly nod. "This story is kind of crazy now." She jostles in her spot to get into a comfortable cross-legged position and leans onto her hand, ready to listen like it's story time in kindergarten. "Okay, so when are you going to meet him?"

I tip my head from side to side. "I'm... not sure I am."

"Why not?"

"I don't know. We live in two different worlds." One where he has millions of dollars and I'm thankful to have received a good mortgage rate.

"He's your father. Don't you want to get to know him? Won't you always wonder?" Deep concern clouds her voice.

"It can't change what happened, I'm no longer a kid."

"No, but we all live longer now, so you're maybe only a quarter through your life. You have seventy-five-percent of your life left that Hudson can be involved in. Don't miss out on that."

"I'm not sure, Luc—"

She growls a noise as she quickly hops off the back of my truck. "You're an idiot."

Quickly, I move to follow her. "Why?"

She grabs chunks of her hair in her hands in frustration. "Do you know how many people would kill to have moments with their parents who *want* to have moments with their kids?"

Shit. I *am* an idiot.

Her parents aren't in her life, not by choice. They were taken too soon, and I know it weighs heavily on her mind.

"Lucy, I'm sorry. I can understand why you may feel that way."

She shakes her disapproval at me. "You'll regret it if you don't meet him. Because we will always regret when we don't have more time with someone. Well, unless you're an asshole, because then I would very much like to re-write those moments."

My jaw flexes side to side. "Ready to switch conversation topics?"

Her hands find her hips. "Only if you give Hudson a chance, because you will *always* wonder, always."

Stepping closer to her, I tell her what she wants to hear. "How about I write back. No promises, but I'll answer him."

Lucy contemplates by bobbing her head. "Fine. But you have a deadline of Friday."

I reach out my fingertip to touch her shoulder. "Okay." Our eyes meet and it's recognition and safety rolled into one. "Ding-ding, round two, your turn."

She huffs out a breath. "I went on a date during spring break, showed up to class the next week, and he was our new

TA, and the asshole made my class hell. Which on top of an already high course load was not what I needed. There you go." Lucy doesn't look at me, maybe because my brain goes through a hundred images of what they may have done on their date. Instead, she walks away then stops to look across the field with her arms folded.

Inside I'm battling the rage I have for this man who I want to kill with my hands. Partly because I'm jealous if he got to kiss her lips, but mostly, how the fuck dare he treat her like a side dish?! Not when Lucy should always be the woman that a guy opens doors for and buys her roses.

Biting the inside of my cheek, I remind myself that now isn't the time to show my emotions. Walking to her, I gently place my hand on her shoulder. "Lucy, forget about him. He isn't worthy of you, and he sure as hell doesn't have a moral compass. I mean, can't he get into a lot of trouble for what happened?"

"He didn't know I was a student, and I didn't know who he was. It was a consensual one... I mean, I never do that kind of thing." I hate that she feels she needs to justify it, just as much as I despise that I'm becoming privy to the details of *that part* of her life.

Squeezing her shoulder, I draw her attention to me. "Don't let him win—"

She cuts me off and shakes her shoulder to release herself from my touch. "You think I would let him be the reason I quit? Am I proud of what happened? No. Did it make me re-think men and my life choices? Yes. A silver lining."

"So what's the real reason you're quitting?"

"I need a break. I feel so... burned out. I can't keep pushing forward, Drew. I'm tired and exhausted. If one more person asks me if I'm taking an extra class or what I will do when I graduate, then I may just burst." She kicks a stone lying in the grass then peers up at me. "Don't you ever just want a moment to breathe?"

A soft smile plays on my lips as I lean down to pick up another stone. "I do." Standing up again, I throw the stone into the far-off distance. "So you want a break then maybe will head back to college?"

"No. I'm not sure college is for me. I have something that I'm working on, and maybe if that goes to plan then I don't need a degree anyway." Using her foot, she draws a circle around her body.

I sigh. I know she has said enough and that I shouldn't push it, but curiosity gets the better of me. "Something going to plan?"

Her mouth finally cracks into a smile. "A secret for now. Don't worry, no men involved, or anyone for that matter." Lucy seems more at ease and her shoulders lower. "I guess we're all shared out—or is there a third round?"

I indicate with my head to the truck. "I think we have mini-apple pie bites still."

"Now that is certainly a way to wrap up this convo." She nearly skips back to my truck.

Following her, we take a few seconds to get comfortable, and I search for the small bag of bites and offer her one, which she gladly takes.

"We are keepers of each other secrets." She examines the piece of pie that is more like a small pastry bar.

"It seems that way." I lick my thumb that is now covered in apple goo. "But your brothers will figure out something is up."

Her brows rise then fall. "Don't I know it, but let me enjoy a week or two of peace."

"Fine."

We both look off at the horizon as the sun begins to sink

lower to the west. The orange light contrasting with the lush green fields are a combo pleasant to the eyes.

Lucy scrunches up a napkin and throws it into the paper bag. Then she does something that surprises me, she rests her head against my shoulder.

"I might skip the whole dating-my-TA detail when I tell my brothers," she casually explains.

"Probably a good plan."

Fuck, why does her hair have to brush the skin of my neck? It's smooth, soft, and is all the persuasion I need to pull her closer. But I'm holding on strong and keep my hand resting on my *own* thigh.

A long silence overtakes us as we just sit there in the moment.

"This is what we used to do, talk and stare. Do you remember?" Her voice is soft and almost whimsical.

My head moves only an inch, but it's enough for my nose to gently graze the top of her head, as if she were mine. "How could I forget?" I faintly whisper. Inside I want to scream that it's on my mind every damn day.

But Lucy being Lucy, she takes us there. "*So*… unless you plan on having your way with me in the back of your truck, then I should probably get back to Grayson's."

I snort a laugh and shake my head, pulling back. "Lucy," I warn.

"What?" she plays innocent. "I'm just presenting options." Her joke is half-serious.

"I'm not answering anything, get in the car."

She grins as we clean up, and a few minutes later, we are back on the road. A song is playing on the speakers, Noah Reid's "False Alarms." The whole premise is about wanting to fall in love, but you can't, and it's perfectly fitting in this moment. We drive for a little while in silence until Lucy breaks it.

"A goat."

I side-eye her with a perplexed look. "Say what?"

Lucy leans against the window and seems to be in deep thought. "They should have gotten Rosie a goat. That's fun, different, and less maintenance than a horse. Plus, with a goat you can have goat yoga workshops or something. Instead, everyone is gushing over Cosmo 2.0."

"Still bitter about that? And it's Astro."

She rolls her eyes and flashes me an unamused look.

"Does it really bother you? Why are you thinking about it now?"

She debates what to say as we approach Grayson's house. "Because I need a distraction when I'm around you and goats seemed like a safe option."

Turning onto the long driveway, I feel heavy. Mostly because I understand her theory, and I wonder if we will always feel this way.

Pulling up behind Brooke's SUV, I turn the engine off and angle my body toward Lucy.

"Goats." I repeat her word and lean over to turn the music down. "I guess this is your stop... thanks for this afternoon."

Her hand lands on the handle but stills. "Likewise. I feel a little lighter—well, maybe not because of our meal choice, but lighter in mind anyways. Would have been better if you told me you wrote me a song or something, but next time, right?" she jokes, but if only she knew that I already have one or two.

Lucy Blisswood is my muse, and if she ever found out then she would never let me forget it.

I smack my lips together and pull them into my mouth as I pat the steering wheel. She takes it as her cue to leave, and she opens the door before glancing over her shoulder. "If you want, I'll go with you when you meet him. Your father, I mean."

"I'm a big boy, Lucy, and I haven't said I'll meet him yet," I volley back.

She gives me a reassuring smile. "You will, because eventually, you'll realize that you deserve to have everything."

Her words hit me in the center of my chest.

"Lucy," I call out before she closes the door. She looks at me with interest. "It's Wednesday. The night I'm playing at Rooster Sin."

A sinfully sexy smile forms on her mouth. "Good to know. I'll need to check my calendar, you know, busy schedule and all."

I shake my head gently, glaring at her, entertained. The moment she closes the door, I curse to myself.

Why did I just volunteer myself for a night of torture? Probably because if I can't have her, then seeing her is the next best thing.

6

DREW

I drag the sandpaper along the long piece of wood as I lean over the table that I created. I use my eyes and fingers to examine where I need to smooth the surface before I glance up. I see that I have Grayson studying me. He's standing in the doorway of the open barn at Olive Owl.

I return to my study of the wood. "Yes?"

"Nothing, just..." He walks a few steps into the barn before resting his hands on his hips. From his tone of voice, I already know that he will have one of his sentimental spiels coming up. "Everything okay?"

Yep, there we are.

Standing up and throwing the paper on the table, I lie. "Perfectly."

A knowing smirk forms at the corner of his mouth. "Really? Because you've been a little different the last few weeks. I mean, don't get me wrong, your work is top-notch. We're ahead on the construction, the crew loves you, and the craftsmanship of this side project is..." He whistles. "Something just seems to be on your mind lately."

My hand comes up to swipe along my chin. "Nah, all good."

Slowly he nods an *okay*. "You know you can tell me anything, right? I mean, if you need anything, just ask," he reminds me in a caring way. Whether it's an ear to listen or financial help, he would step up without a doubt.

"I know, Grayson, and I appreciate everything you do. But it's all good," I lie, because if I tell him about Hudson then it will be a long conversation, and then he'll ask me a hundred times more if I'm okay before he has Brooke whipping up cookies to send to me. Nor can I tell him that his younger sister is on a carousel ride in my head.

Grayson holds his hands up in surrender. "All right, just thought I would ask." He circles around the table, admiring my carvings on the legs. "You're going to sell this? You could get a lot."

"Haven't thought that far. It was more of a pastime."

He throws me a funny look. "You said that about the bookshelf you created a few months ago too, then sold it at the farmers' market for a solid amount."

My lips twitch as if a proud smile is too timid to come out.

A few beats pass before he speaks again. "Can I ask you something else?"

"Sure."

Shit, I know what's coming.

I bite my lip to try to contain my dislike for what he is about to ask, but I know it deep within my bones.

"Lucy…"

Uh-huh, here we go.

"Is something up with her? I mean, I feel like I'm not getting the whole story. She's your friend, and I know you two have hung out over the years. I thought maybe she would have mentioned something in the past few days or yesterday when she was with you. I'm worried."

Fuck, why did he have to add in the worried proclamation?

I hate myself right now. He is the last person that I should be hiding information from and lying to, but that's all I seem to be doing this week.

I raise both of my hands to rest on the back of my head as I stretch my body casually. "Your guess is as good as mine. Why, is she acting odd at home?"

Grayson snorts a laugh. "Truthfully, I haven't noticed, partly because with the kids and Lucy in her room studying, then we haven't had a lot of chances to catch up. Just something inside of me feels like there is more behind why she's back. I love having her here, but yeah."

"Sorry, man, I don't have much insight."

Grayson nods and heads back outside. "Thanks. But if you learn anything new then—"

"I'll let you know."

His appreciative smile feels like it may kill me. I'm definitely relieved that I'm boxing later, as I need to work out some stress.

My phone lights up where it's lying on the table, and when I unlock the screen, I see it's only a junk email with pizza coupons. But it gets me to an inbox where I have an email sitting in draft. I tap my finger on the screen but avoid the send button as my jaw flexes side to side.

What the hell, I should just do it. This week has already taken a few twists.

Fuck it. I hit send.

———

"FUCK, WHAT'S GOTTEN INTO YOU?" Knox asks. He's feeling the brunt of my punches as he holds the pads up, and we move across the grass near a field of grapes. Pretzel the dog watches from the side as he sits and pants.

Nothing like a warm afternoon and boxing to get out some tension.

"Nothing, just want to have a good workout. If you can't handle it, then that's not my problem." I deliver an uppercut with my gloved hand.

Knox flashes his eyes at me because he's entertained by my words. "Wake up on the wrong side of the bed this morning? You know I can take you down if I need to."

Stilling my shuffling feet, I give up for a moment. This isn't the mind frame any of us needs.

Knox throws the pads to the side and picks up his water bottle. I do the same.

"It isn't Lucy, is it? I mean the reason you seem a little extra tense?" Knox's words surprise me, partly because I hear an undercurrent of a hint.

Then again, I haven't done anything with Lucy that would land me in the Blisswood doghouse.

"Come on, we all know Lucy had a little crush on you when she was a teenager. Now you're both grown adults, and single. Around one another a lot too. Friends, sure, but I know you look at her like a little sister, and no matter what Lucy does, you won't go there. I know you worry about her the same way we do," he explains.

What is with today? Now I'm getting the reminder that Lucy is very much off-limits. I can't even correct him that no, no I don't see her like a little sister. I wish I could, but she's anything but.

I blink a few times, and I only nod. "Just a long week, you know?"

"It's Tuesday," he replies point-blank.

Taking a long sip from my water bottle, I hum a sound. "Exactly, we still have more than half the week ahead. Anyways, how are you and Madison?" Diversion works with Knox, so that's what I do.

"All good. The school year just finished, so she has vacation all summer from teaching. Makes lunchtime more fun." A devilish look forms on his face and I can only imagine what he means.

Shaking my head, I look around to admire the clear blue skies and summer afternoon. But from the corner of my eye, I've already captured the movement of a pair of legs in boots and way-too-short shorts.

Lucy approaches us with her ponytail wagging with her sway. Our eyes catch, but only for a moment, as she chooses to focus on Knox—a good choice, a safe choice.

"Hey, Knox, I think Cosmo 2.0 needs his hooves trimmed earlier than planned."

"Really going to avoid calling him Astro?" Her brother raises a brow.

Lucy reaches up to tighten her hair tie. "Yes. Now, who do we call?"

Knox begins to gather the boxing supplies. "Ask Grayson. He's responsible for the horse and what Rosie does or doesn't do with the beast. They only house him here."

"Fine. And I couldn't find the key for the closet that has the olive oil bottles that need to be filled."

Knox now looks confused. "Did I miss the memo that you're working here this summer? I mean, don't you have classes?"

Lucy looks slightly panicked for a second and her eyes slide over to me before back to Knox. She rolls a shoulder back. "I said I would help out when I can," she says, her tone reminding him—or correcting him, but either way it's full of attitude.

"Fine. Be my guest at making yourself useful." Knox hauls the gym bag he packed over his shoulder and begins to walk toward the main house with Pretzel following in tow. "Drew, don't forget poker night this weekend. I demand a rematch after you won last time," he calls out to me over his shoulder before disappearing.

Lucy is quick to leave, but I stop her by grabbing her arm.

"You may need to put in a little more effort to show that everything is swell with you. All afternoon your brothers have been bothering me, and now you look like a woman who is distracting herself."

She pulls her arm away, clearly annoyed. "I *am* distracting myself." Lucy groans and swipes some hair out of her face. "Sorry, didn't mean to snap, just didn't sleep well last night."

"Everything okay?" Concern is evident in my voice as I stare at her intently.

She laughs, sounding nearly sinister. "Surely you must be able to relate? Want to tell me that you honestly slept last night?" Her voice has a sultry tone that warns me she wants to taunt me in the next thirty seconds.

"Lucy," I plead and quickly scan the area to ensure that nobody is watching. She jabs her finger into my chest, and when I look down, I need to attack my bottom lip with my teeth to keep myself in check. Then I decide to change our direction of conversation. "I did it."

When I pull my phone from my pocket, it causes her finger to drop, and I use my thumbprint to unlock the screen and hold out my phone.

With interest, Lucy grabs the phone and reads the email aloud.

Hi. I got your letter. We can meet, just let me know what dates work for you. -Drew.

"That's it?" She glances up from the screen with a funny look.

"Yeah. What do you mean that's it?"

She snorts a cute little laugh. "It's very… minimal."

"I'm not an English major," I justify and take my phone back.

"Okay, I mean, I guess when you meet in person then you can get to know him. For now, this works." Her face softens as her eyes offer reassurance. "You did it, and before our deadline."

I grin, almost proud. "Yep, so your turn. You need to tell your brothers."

She rolls her eyes at the reminder. "I know, I'm just waiting for something to give me the courage, a sign or something. But I'll do it, okay."

"Fine. Well, I'll see you around, okay?"

Her playful look returns. "Tomorrow, actually."

Right, because torturing me is her favorite pastime.

"I'm trying to figure out what I'm going to wear tomorrow for Rooster Sin. Tough life choices, really." She steps closer. "I mean, the dress with thin straps that requires no bra or the tank top where you can see my bra?"

I close then open my eyes, trying desperately to scrape the image from my brain. But like the idiot I am, my mouth opens. "Tank top."

Her eyes brighten with surprise, as she wasn't expecting me to say anything, and hell, it surprises me too.

A hopeful hint of a smirk spreads on her mouth. "A good thing I get to live a little before I share my news with everyone."

Then she walks away, taking my resolve with her.

LUCY

Grabbing my bottle of beer from the bar, I scan the busy dive bar.

"It's funny they carded you, even though they know who you are," my friend Kendall mentions as she drinks from her cola, as she is the designated driver tonight.

I glance to the side at her as I stand and lean against the bar to ensure I have a perfect view of the little stage and the full audience sitting at tiny tables. "It's the law, they have to."

"True. Your brothers are coming tonight?"

"Nah, not this time. It was chaos when I left Grayson's house, and I can only imagine that it's worse at Bennett's house with the boys. Maybe Knox will come, but I don't know. Everyone is kind of in their own worlds."

Kendall tightens her high blonde ponytail. "Makes sense. Tomorrow I'm heading up to the suburbs, want to come with? Was going to do a little shopping."

I keep my eyes fixed on the stage. "No, it's okay. Shopping is probably the last thing that I should be doing now. I already know Grayson will tell me that I need to find a job, as the deal was my trust fund was for college and only college."

"Ah, so it could be we're here to avoid the situation, or we are here because your favorite man just stepped up onto stage with his guitar, and you're wearing a hot outfit." She flashes me a knowing smirk.

Surveying myself, I admire how this simple dress with thin spaghetti straps does me justice. It's casual, but the fit makes me feel like a million bucks. I know Drew said tank top in his momentary lapse of self-control that I will never let him forget, yet I can't get too excited either. Anyways, I never listen, so I went with the dress.

I watch Drew with interest as he sits on a chair with his guitar to tune a few strings. The lighting in this place is dim, but there's a spotlight on him, with a green backdrop.

I've seen Drew a few times playing guitar, normally just casually when he was hanging out with my brothers, but never like this, not with all the attention on him. He normally hates that kind of stuff.

But staring at him now, he looks like a man confident and at ease. His black t-shirt and jeans completely hug his body, and my attraction only seems to grow; nor does that surprise me.

Kendall clears her throat. Obviously, I just checked out into my own world where I was admiring Drew and probably look like a woman with a schoolgirl crush.

"Sorry, I guess…"

She nudges my arm with her shoulder. "It's okay, I know you're using me as your wing woman for tonight. I'll let it slide since we've been friends for years and half of that time you've been pining over him. But now that you're back and older, what are the actual chances that you and him, well…"

I scoff a laugh. "Low, sadly. He will always be more loyal to my brothers than me. Every time over the years that I've tried to get a taste of what it would be like between us, he just ensures I get the hint that nothing will ever happen. And even when his eyes say one thing, his actions say another. It's pretty clear I'm supposed to be off-limits."

It's like trying to break a big rock or tearing down a mountain. You can't. Instead, you may need a volcano or some seismic event to reshape the outlook.

"Do you think if your brothers weren't in the picture that you and he would have a chance?"

I stop my gawking and turn around to face the bar and look to my friend on the side. "I don't know. That's the big mystery. We have a connection, but he has never given me a confirmation that I'm not losing my mind. We just sort of, I guess, click every time we see one another, maybe the occasional flirty statement, but the man is like a stone sometimes. I may chase, and he will silently watch."

"Hmmm, well, maybe this summer you will get your answer."

Commotion begins in the bar, and I glance over my shoulder to see that people are welcoming Drew to the stage now that he's ready.

"Seems like your rock star has a fan club," Kendall teases me in a playful tone.

Both of us move to get a good position to view Drew.

"Hi, everyone," he says into the microphone as he adjusts the guitar on his lap. "I guess most of you know me by now." People from the crowd whistle. "I perform every now and then." Somebody howls out an indistinguishable word. Drew looks down at his instrument then back up, with his eyes squinting as if he is searching through the light. "Sometimes I do covers, but I also have my own stuff."

"We want a Drew Mac original," someone shouts out. It causes that wry smile to spread on Drew's face, the one I love the most. It's a cross between polite, but shows he has an opinion in his head that he will never share.

"The plan was to do some covers first." There is a moment of pause as our eyes catch. I make no mistake that our eyes lock, with my heart jumping in the process. His Adam's apple bobs as he swallows. Then he peers down to the strings of his guitar. "You know what, fuck it. An original it is."

Great, I get to listen to him croon over some girl who probably broke his heart. But I'll listen because I can't tear my eyes away from him even if I tried.

The sound of a guitar strum fills the room for a few notes before turning into a melody.

Then he sings into the mic.

> *Long nights, no light, something ain't right.*
> *It's your blue eyes.*
> *They send my mind into a fight.*
> *Every time I look away, it's a lie.*
> *But you're out of reach anyway.*
> *Thoughts of you are all I get.*
> *And I hit repeat, again and again.*

I listen and admire his talent. But something stirs inside of me, awakens an instinct that I should listen more closely.

"Blue-eyed girl is lucky if she gets a song," Kendall quips, and I only gently raise the corner of my mouth in acknowledgment.

Because as Drew heads into his chorus, a hope inside me slowly dissolves into something new.

> *You'll show up to my door, wanting your way.*

My body freezes when he mentions showing up to his door. It can't be, must be a coincidence. A general phrase to rhyme in his song. No way a reference to my eighteen-year-old self's indiscretion. But I'm already drawn in and convinced.

> *You'll lie there, beautiful as always.*
> *You'll be everything that I see, until I go blind.*
> *In my mind you'll stay, in my arms together entwined.*
> *But I'm not the answer you need.*
> *So in my mind you'll stay.*

The song goes on, and my ability to blink is gone. I feel it deep within my bones that he is singing about me. Especially when he sings more.

> *Long rides, no words, something ain't right.*
> *It's your blue eyes.*
> *They send us onto a long road.*
> *Every time I look away, I look back.*
> *Just like you never do as you're told.*
> *But you're still out of reach anyways.*
> *Thoughts of you are all I get,*
> *And I hit repeat, again and again.*

I stand there, frozen, as all these little references seem to resemble us. Showing up at his door, car rides, blue eyes. For the next few songs, my mind is in a muddled fog. He plays a few covers, but it doesn't matter, the spark already ignited when he sang his own song… about me.

It all registers with me, and it feels like my blood is speeding through my body. I stand there, speechless and in awe. This can't be my mind playing tricks on me, or so I pray that it isn't the case. Because it can't be a mistake that his song, his original song that he wrote, is about me. And if that's the case, then what he wants is exactly what I've hoped for all these years.

All these years.

Something inside of me wants to snap, cry, or rejoice. I'm not crazy, but I've been waiting, when all along he feels the same, yet he pushed me away.

Heat flushes through my body, and I recognize that I need air. Standing here listening to the man of my dreams confirm we want the same thing has my heart growing or breaking, it hasn't been decided, but neither is good for me right now.

"I'll be right back, just need the ladies' room," I mumble to my friend, and I beeline it to the bathroom as everyone claps; his set is over. Avoiding the bathroom, I take a detour to the exit and emerge into the parking lot. It's not yet pitch-dark, but it is very gray, as a dark cloud looms in the west. We're getting a cold front tonight.

The humid air makes this situation worse. I feel like I can't breathe. There are droplets of rain, and everything is sticky and warm, but still better than being inside at this very moment.

"Lucy!"

I whip my head around to see Drew standing there, his eyes as stormy as the sky. We're both breathing heavy, our chests bouncing up and down.

Marching forward, I have no hesitation, and my palms land on his chest to push him. "It was about me, wasn't it? The song." I don't need to clarify because his eyes tell me enough. His lids squeeze shut then pop open, maybe with remorse or with his own revelation that he can't avoid this anymore. He stays mute, which causes me to claw his shirt. "Tell me," I plead in a whisper.

"It's going to pour rain any minute, we should go inside."

"No. Not until you tell me." I remain adamant and our eyes connect. "You knew I was listening."

His lips roll in before his mouth opens as something snaps inside of him. "Fuck it, you're right, okay?"

"Then say it," I demand for the last time.

He brings his hands to encircle gently around my wrists. "It's about you."

My entire heart sinks and blossoms. I'm left speechless as we stand there, with droplets of rain picking up pace.

"Lucy, let's just go—"

"No, you're an asshole! I get the confirmation that you feel the same way as I do, and you just want me to forget it?" A tint of dismay and anger comes through my tone.

He nearly smirks at me. "It's beginning to pour, Lucy, so yes, let's go inside and forget this."

I laugh bitterly at him as I grip his shirt tighter. "You really think I'm going to do that?"

He stares at my mouth, desperate and curious. "No, I don't, but you've been drinking and I'm not going to kiss you drunk."

"I had half of a beer, I'm perfectly aware of what is happening. Wait, you want to kiss me?" I may be aware, but my mind is getting lost in this situation. Especially as it begins to pour, causing our clothes to get soaked within seconds, and the sound of nature is drowning my ears.

Drew steps closer to me, moving to cradle my head in his hands. "Lucy, this can't happen," he reminds us, but he makes no effort to look away.

"For once, make us stop wondering," I speak up, trying to battle my voice with the volume of the rain.

"Lucy," he mutters.

But not for long, because his mouth crashes down on my

own, stealing my breath with his. I don't even hesitate. If this is my only chance, then I'm going to get every second he'll give.

His kiss is bruising, but then his lips soften, and his tongue runs along the line of my lips before dipping into my mouth. The feeling of my body surrendering to him holds me down, just as his hand slides to the back of my neck to keep me in his hold.

It's a caress, his tongue. Maybe he thinks I'm fragile or maybe he's trying to trace my every inch to imprint in his memory. My hands and arms fall free as I give up on any feelings of anger, because one kiss with Drew and it's worth the wait. Encircling my arms up around his neck, I selfishly want to keep him closer to me.

Our lips brush as we inhale a breath before reuniting for a deeper kiss. The type of kiss that scares me.

Because this isn't just a dream, it's a new fact; Drew is the last man that I'll ever kiss.

In his arms, his lips on mine, this feeling is proof that I don't want anyone else. He may think this is our only kiss, but my soul knows that he is the only man that I'll ever kiss again.

I'm his.

Reluctantly we both pull away. Our eyes connect in realization of what we just did, because we can't take it back.

Droplets of rain slide down our faces. My finger instantly comes up to shush his mouth. I don't want him to ruin this moment, and he doesn't, because he escapes my finger and kisses my forehead tenderly.

"Don't think. Don't say it," I nearly pant, as my entire body feels like I just finished a marathon, with my adrenaline high. "I'm not your regret."

"That was anything but." He seems to be in a daze. "That's the problem." It comes out hoarse.

I step back, not ready for this to end, but I need to safeguard my heart from further expectations. "I guess taking me back to your place is off the table?" I blankly quip.

He looks away then back at me, a hint of a smile on his face. "It is." Then his manner changes and he holds my face in his hands so I can't look away. "You're not a regret. You're not a mistake. And fuck, I wish I could do more. But this is us. Here in the rain, our moment, and now I need to figure out what the hell to do. I need to stay away from you, but maybe I'm more selfish than I think."

I nod, as I comprehend that he is asking for time or space, anything to try and get a grip on his thoughts, which I can relate to.

"Now get inside, Lucy, then go home. Do that for me," he requests, and like a fool, I nod again, because I'm drunk on the feeling of his lips planted on my own.

Slowly I walk out of his hold, his hand letting go of me at the very end. Why am I so compliant?

Probably because tomorrow is looking more hopeful.

8
LUCY

He kissed me. He finally kissed me.

I haven't shed this giddy look on my face since I woke up this morning. A constant replay has been streaming in my head all day. Luckily, I slept in, which means I missed Grayson or Brooke this morning, as they had things to do. A soft squeal escapes from my mouth as I turn off the engine to my car that I just parked at Olive Owl.

I'm still on a high from last night, with endorphins making me feel temporarily fearless. Which is why I am here to find Knox to tell him my college news; I figured he would be the most accepting of my brothers and will help me break the news to Grayson and Bennett.

I grab my phone from the drink holder and quickly check on the screen for any new emails, but sadly nothing thrilling has come in since the last time I checked, which was two hours ago during my morning coffee.

Sliding out of my car, I take a deep breath of the fresh-smelling air. The humidity has disappeared, and everything feels clear.

Walking toward the side of the house, with the sound of my sandals flopping, I laugh when I see Madison leaning down cooing at the dog, rubbing Pretzel's belly, his legs straight in the air and his face showing pure delight.

Madison peeks up at me. "I know, he has me wrapped around his paws. I've been at this for five minutes after I massaged his ears."

I join her by squatting down to pet the canine's fur. "It's okay, we all know you're only with my brother for the dog," I joke, and she smiles in response.

"Everything good with you? I heard you looked like fire last night." Madison flashes her brows at me, and I look at her, confused about how she would know. "Brooke may have sent a group text to Kelsey and me, wondering if we had any intel as to why you looked smoking hot."

"It was just an outfit and… nothing special," I lie, but I want to scream that Drew and I finally kissed.

Once, in high school, Madison overheard me telling Kendall my plan to try and seduce Drew. I was only seventeen at the time, and she subtly let me know that it wasn't a good idea in her ever-so-relatable teacher tone. Instead, I waited until I was eighteen to try my plan…

"Rooster Sin, right?" she checks, and I already know she has a theory in her head.

"Yes, *with Kendall.*"

Madison pats Pretzel one last time, before standing, and I follow suit. Pretzel instantly flips to his belly and shakes off before standing, and he goes well past my waist in size.

Madison pulls her long blonde hair to the side. "Everything okay, Lucy?" Her sincere caring voice comes out.

With a slight struggle, I smile. "Sure, why wouldn't it be?"

"Lucy." Her teacher tone hits me in my weak spot.

I sigh. "Actually… is Knox around? I came to talk to him."

Her hand comes to touch my shoulder. "He is, but…" Madison seems uncomfortable. "He's not alone."

My brothers.

"Grayson and Bennett are here, aren't they?" A low growl rumbles deep in my throat.

Madison's awkward look confirms it. "They've been talking out back for a good hour."

"How bad is it?" I ask, slightly afraid.

She shrugs. "No clue, but I've heard your name mentioned a few times."

"Great," I sarcastically answer with dread.

"Come find me after if you need anything."

I nod before walking slowly toward my demise. Circling around the house, I find my brothers sitting on the patio in deep conversation. That is until Bennett looks up to see me, and the rest of the pack follows his gaze.

I'm walking into the lion's den, and I know it.

Swallowing, I know it's a stupid question, but I ask anyway. "Am I missing a family vote?" I awkwardly joke.

Grayson leans back in the chair with arms crossed. "Your landlord phoned me to ask if you would be ending the lease for the start of the new academic year or mid-summer, because he mentioned you said you wouldn't be staying," he states.

My face immediately drops. Grayson is responsible for anything financial related to school, so I guess the landlord reached out.

I need to just rip the band-aid off. "Because I'm not staying."

"What do you mean?" Bennett asks. "You have one semester left since you took all of those extra courses the last few years." His tone is apprehensive, and his face shows me he isn't happy with my news.

"Well, I'm not going to finish." I stand strong and firm in my choice, my feet remaining rooted to the ground.

"Explain, Lucy," Grayson requests.

"I don't think it's for me. I don't have the energy to continue, so I've made a choice," I softly inform him, choosing to leave out all the million reasons that I could come up with.

Knox quickly pipes up, "Then take time off and then start again." His adamancy surprises me, as I thought he would be the one on my team. "You are so close to the finish line, you'll regret it." Disappointment floods his face before his eyes draw a line from me down to the ground, as if he is unable to look at me right now.

Shaking my head, I snicker a sound because I'm annoyed. "I can't believe this. A Blisswood family meeting that is yet again about what to do with Lucy. I'm allowed to make decisions too."

"Sure, but this is a stupid one," Bennet tells me. "Dad wouldn't be happy about it, and you put in so much work that, of course, we're not going to let you make a mistake. So don't throw in the dramatics." He stretches out his legs, crosses his ankles, and leans into his propped elbow.

Grayson motions for him to simmer down, but then turns his attention to me. "What's going on? Is there something we should be worried about? This isn't like you. A college degree was your dream."

"Dreams change," I reply simply. Walking a few steps to the long lounge chair, I flop down on the end.

There is a long silence as everyone seems to be stewing in my unacceptable choice.

"Grayson's right, what aren't you telling us?" Bennett seems to have cooled down slightly.

My shoulder slants up toward my ear, and my mouth quirks as I debate how to get out of this conversation. Honesty may be the best policy, but I'm not sure we're all ready for the emotional discussion that we eventually need to have, the one we've avoided for years. Because losing both parents does something to you, yet we all moved on like everything is dandy, but eventually, loss can catch up with you.

"In the last five years, I've done everything that was asked of me. Didn't blink an eye when Grayson became occupied with his new family, was nothing but positive when Bennett accidentally got Kelsey pregnant, and you." I look at Knox who briefly glances up at me. "I stayed on your team when you decided pursuing my teacher was a grand idea. You have all gotten everything you dreamed of, all while I worked my ass off, with extra courses and deadlines. I'm…" I remember briefly the kiss from last night, and it acts as a form of encouragement. Sometimes you need something amazing to handle the not-so-stellar moments. "I'm worn out, and I'm not convinced college is for me or that it will get me to where I need to go."

Bennett scoffs before he rubs his hands over his face. "Where you need to go? Are you kidding me? Lucy, you are capable of so many things, which is why I don't understand that you can't see that holding out a little longer to complete your degree will open so many more doors."

"She needs a break, so let her have a break," Knox snaps at Bennett.

I appreciate his intervention, but now I need to deliver the other news. "I can't defer. Or rather, I would need to re-apply later. It's either I finish now or lose my spot in the program."

Grayson stands up. "Bullshit. I'll phone the dean and tell him that it's unacceptable."

I roll my eyes in annoyance. "Jesus, Grayson, a call with the dean just doesn't happen at the snap of your fingers, nor are people there like people here in Bluetop, they couldn't care less that you're a Blisswood."

"I'll send a crate of wine," he adds.

"Great, let's add bribery to that bad scenario," I retort.

Knox groans. "Maybe we all sit on this for a day or two before regrouping?"

"Fine, but if she doesn't go back to college, then we need to come up with a plan B," Bennett states, and it infuriates me.

"I'm right here, confident that I should have a say." I wave my hands to draw their attention to me.

Bennett flashes me a contrite smile. "Sure, when you tell me how you plan to pay for adulthood, then I'm all ears."

"Are you kidding me right now? Why do you have to be such an asshole? You've always been the cuddly bear type of brother," I argue back.

Immediately his demeanor changes to a more sympathetic approach. "You're right, I'm sorry. I've been lacking sleep these days, and I'm not sure how to handle this."

Looking around at my brothers, I know this isn't what they signed up for. Raising me was handed to them, and they stepped up without question. None of us want to be in this situation.

And here I am, not making it any easier for them.

"It feels like you're still not telling us something," Grayson reiterates as he glances off into the rows of grapevines.

"It doesn't matter. I'm here, and this is my choice."

"Let's leave this for now, we all need to let it sink in,"

Knox suggests again, which feels like my brother has softened over the years.

"Fine, you're right," Bennett agrees. "But, Lucy, we're here for you. Doesn't mean we agree with your decision," he remains firm in his stance.

Knox stands up, clearly done with this conversation. "He's right. I'll be damned if we turn our backs, but I think you're making a mistake." Knox then walks off back into the house.

My eyes travel to Grayson, who sighs. "We'll talk about it tomorrow. I need to sleep on this and talk with Brooke." He plays with the wedding ring on his finger. "Let's try and have a normal dinner tonight with the kids, okay?" His tone is soft and comforting.

"It's okay, I don't think I'll be around for dinner." I tuck a strand of hair behind my ear. "I'll probably hang with Kendall since she's starting an internship next week."

Bennett huffs a laugh. "Right. Heaven help me, but I'm actually going to say look at Kendall as an example," he wisecracks before he too stands and leaves.

It feels like another punch. How many times can I be reminded of their disapproval of my choice?

Grayson walks to me and stops. Blowing out a breath, he studies me. "Why did you wait to tell us?"

I laugh at his question. "Did you not just witness the last ten minutes? Maybe that's why."

The line of his mouth stretches slightly as he clearly understands. He slaps a hand on my shoulder before leaving me alone on the patio.

My throat tightens as the realization of how much disappointment I've brought to them hits me harder than I thought. I suddenly feel small and know they all look at me differently.

Good God, it will feel worse when their wives feel the need to seek me out to try and comfort me.

I need to get out of here, and that's exactly what I do.

————

THE DOORBELL IS NEW, or at least it wasn't here last time. This isn't where Drew lived when I was eighteen, but I saw this place a year ago before he started working on it.

I wish I could say I feel confident, but I don't. I feel fragile, because telling my brothers was slightly soul-crushing.

The door opens, and Drew can instantly tell I'm not okay, but he doesn't move out of the way, either, as he leans against the pane of the door.

"I told my brothers. It was swell," I mundanely say, and it causes his dimple to appear which informs me he understands my humor. "Okay, it was fucking awful. Or at least that's how I feel."

He crosses his arms. "What are you doing here, Lucy?" His tone is so simple that I can't figure out if he is happy or disdained that I'm standing before him.

All I can do is explain. I begin to shake my head side to side as my emotions build inside of me. "It made sense. I got in my car and it led me to you."

"Do your brothers know you're here?"

"No. I don't know where else to go. Can I stay here tonight?"

His eyes assess my body, traveling up and down, and his face remains neutral which makes me anxiously wait for an answer.

But for the second time this week, a feeling of hope hits me.

Because he steps aside, indicating that I can come in.

9

DREW

I should push her away.

But I sure as hell am not going to let her wander around upset.

Then again, kissing her last night and now letting her spend the night is a direct route to confusion. Because she isn't going to like what I have to say. And my dick won't enjoy my standpoint, either. But I have rules to follow, and a lifetime of weakened resolve to live with.

Lucy steps into my house and already I feel like she's taking all the air from this place, and not in a bad way, either.

Her eyes circle the living room as she steps into my ranch-style house, and I lazily close the door behind me.

"Wow, this place looks amazing. I can tell you put in a lot of work." She seems to be admiring my home as she takes in all the details.

I scratch the back of my head. "Yeah, amazing what a little drywall and new furniture can do."

She sends a gentle smile my way. "It looks good." Her eyes land on my guitar that is leaning against a stand, and fuck me, we're only thirty seconds in and last night is already dancing in our heads.

Our eyes catch and her bottom lip lowers, but she pauses for a second.

This is where I need to step in and give us some guidelines, because I sure as hell am about to lose my mind, as her hair is down today, and I love it when her hair is down.

"Look, Lucy, I can only imagine what the Blisswood family intervention must've felt like. And you can stay here tonight, as I wouldn't want a family dinner with Brooke and Grayson right now either, when I know they would ask if you're okay every thirty seconds and stare at you with concerned eyes. But you can sleep on the futon in the spare room. Are we clear?" I head in the direction of my kitchen off the living room to get us something to drink. I would love to pull out a bottle of Jack, but I need my head to be sharp if Lucy is going to be under my roof. I already had a temporary lapse of judgment last night.

"Okay."

I glance over my shoulder. Lucy doesn't do agreeable, but right now her face is neutral, and she heads to the bar stool at the counter.

I let it go and focus on pouring some water from the fridge.

"What did they say?" I wonder, as I can only assume.

She scoffs. "You know, the usual. 'We don't want you to make a mistake, Lucy.' 'Is there something else going on, Lucy?' 'You'll regret this, Lucy.' Oh, and my personal favorite, 'Give us a few days and then we can discuss what to do.' And don't worry, the disappointment was on all of their faces."

I hand her a glass of water and try to suppress a smile.

Not because it's funny—it's not, and I agree with them—but she just relayed what I knew they would all do.

Leaning against the counter across from her, I debate what to say, as she doesn't need any more lectures.

A long silence overtakes us, and she must pick up on this, because she speaks up in an effort to end it. "Did you hear from Hudson?"

For a second I remember that she's the only one in Bluetop I can talk to about this, as she knows my secret. It is certainly a relief. "I did. He emailed me back asking if we could meet for lunch, and he sent me some dates. We could meet halfway, or I can visit him at his weekend house about an hour and a half from here."

A weekend house; haven't even met the man and already I know he is out of my realm.

"And? Did you respond?" She gives me a curious look, almost as if she's excited for me.

I shrug a shoulder and push my glass of water to the side as I lean over the counter. "Not yet."

I can tell she wants to chuckle. "Typical Drew."

I roll my eyes. I know she gets me, just as I know she won't push further. God, I like the way she just stroked her face to brush a strand of hair to the side. So fucking beautiful, and she's going to be sleeping in my house.

I'm doomed.

"Uhm," I say, and my throat feels dry. "Hungry?" My voice sounds a bit shaky.

Lucy forms a wry smile, because she must know that I'm avoiding the fact that I've replayed kissing her in my head about million times today.

"Sure. Grilled cheese?"

My forehead furrows at her choice. She flashes me a look

before bouncing off the stool. "I figure every bachelor has bread and cheese in their kitchen. Seemed like a safe bet."

I smile at her thought as she heads straight to the fridge, and I lean over to the breadbox to grab the loaf of bread. We meet by the stove, and I think this is the closest that I've been to her since the kiss.

Fuck, I'm not sure we even need to turn on the stove. I'm already feeling heat between us. Partly because she's forbidden, and the other half because in another life, she would be the kind of girl that I would want every day in my kitchen.

"You know the secret to grilled cheese is the amount of butter on the bread and the way you press on it with the spatula. It really gets to me that people don't realize that. I mean, it's like two pieces of bread with cheese stuck in between, how hard can it be?" she says as she gets busy spreading butter on bread and starting the stove.

"Should be simple enough."

She points the spatula at me. "Are you a grilled cheese and ketchup type of person? Because that is the best way to eat it."

I lean sideways against the counter while I watch her cooking in my kitchen. Maybe if I just ignore the world for a few minutes and enjoy the fact she's here, then no harm will be done.

"People underestimate how using whole wheat bread actually adds some flavor to grilled cheese," she continues as she flips a sandwich.

As much as I appreciate her effort to keep us in safe conversation, I'm not sure I want to hear about cheese for the next ten minutes. "Lucy." She glances to her side to meet my piercing gaze that has been taking in the view.

"Yes, Drew." I know that tone; it's sexy and challenging

rolled into one. My ears and cock love it, but my brain screams to ignore it.

"Where do your brothers think you are right now?"

"At Kendall's."

"You're sleeping in the spare room," I remind her.

The corner of her mouth curves up, clearly entertained. "You mentioned."

"Last night. I meant what I said." I'm declaring it more for myself than her, and judging by the look on her face, I know that she doesn't believe it, and nor do I.

Ignoring me, she works on the grilled cheese and cuts the sandwiches in half. Then she steps over to me and brings the food to my mouth to shut me up and taunt me. "Shh. Now eat."

Dinner is excruciating to say the least. She doesn't bring the kiss up, and instead, we talk about music and TV series. Safe topics.

After dinner, we clean up, and I notice Lucy seems a bit drained.

"Everything good?" I ask.

She twirls hair around her finger as she stands against the fridge. "I guess, I just feel bad that I've let my brothers down. They've done so much for me, and now it seems like I've slapped them in the face. I hate it."

I close the dishwasher. "You're lucky, Lucy. They care beyond the world for you."

"I know. You know, maybe Hudson will be like that. Have you thought about it? I mean, what kind of relationship you want with him?" she innocently asks.

I sigh as I consider what has been bouncing in my head. "I haven't thought that far." It's the truth. "I need to meet him first before thinking about what comes next. But I don't know, I doubt we have much in common. He has a weekend house, for crying out loud."

Lucy gives me a peculiar look as her hands come to her hips. "And? Who cares? You don't care about money."

"Because I don't exactly have a bank account in Panama," I quip.

"I think you're just trying to find a reason not to like him. But you know you're allowed to have someone who wants to give you the world. Everyone deserves that."

She sounds so sure of herself when she declares that theory, and there are a few times in my life when she has made me feel like it could be true. After all, she never gave up on me when we were younger, which is partly why her brothers let me into their world in the first place.

"Maybe." I stop before the words hit my tongue, but then I look at her watching me intently. "I don't want him to feel guilty for the life I was dealt, or maybe he will disappoint me, or I'll disappoint him, and then I can add him to the list of people who are a letdown."

Lucy immediately pounces forward and touches my face with her fingertips. "That's their loss, not yours. They would be lucky to have you in their life, and either way, you have people who love you." I wonder if she means her family or her.

"You're so sure of yourself."

A smirk crawls on her lips. "Because I know it's the truth. Why else wouldn't you have told my brothers about Hudson?"

"What do you mean?"

"Unlucky for me, my brothers are as much your brothers. Friends, sure, but I know you feel indebted to Grayson when you shouldn't, because he truly does love having you in his life, and you don't want him to feel like someone will swoop in and replace him in that family role." She steps closer to me, taking her pointer finger and tapping my chest as if that's the icing on the cake to her philosophy.

My body tightens from her touch. It craves more, and warning signs flare in my head. I adjust my neck, trying to get a comfortable stance—no luck. "You're smart, Lucy, way too smart. Exactly why you shouldn't give up on college."

Her confidence sags, and her face drops at the reminder. "Don't start with me. Or I will just bring up the kiss."

Immediately, I grab her arm. "Lucy, not a good idea. It is what it is."

"Is it?" Her eyes widen. "You knew full well I was listening, yet you sang that song, and then you kissed me. Why would you do that?"

"Because since you've been back, I'm not thinking clearly. Maybe it's because of this Hudson stuff or it's simply that you're here. The moment I saw your smile again, I felt less lost," I admit with conviction in my voice. "We're friends first, let's just leave it at that." It's a plea that I know will fall on deaf ears, but at least I can say I tried.

She looks at me, almost amused. "We were never friends." I look at her, confused, and she goes on to clarify. "Every time I return to Bluetop on the rare occasion, you and I reconnect in an odd way. Sometimes I swear I don't need to say anything and you understand. Since the moment I laid eyes on you, I knew you were something special. I just need you to believe that it's worth it." Her eyes land on my hand where I'm touching her arm.

I notice her breath moving in and out of her chest, and my own breath is heavy. I'm fighting my hands wanting to pull her in tight against my chest.

"Lucy." I want to scream that I would give her my heart

willingly if I knew it would all be worth it, but she deserves more. "Goats."

Her eyes flash up to meet mine, and a knowing smirk forms due to my use of our escape word, and she gently nods to let me off the hook.

"So, tell me about this spare room?" I hear the annoyance in her tone, which makes me smile.

I tip my head in the direction of the hall, and we walk. I show her the bathroom, thankful I never touch the spare bathroom, and grab fresh linens from the hall closet. While she makes her bed, I grab a spare t-shirt from my room and sigh, knowing that she will be sleeping in the other room while wearing my shirt.

When I walk to the door of the spare room, she's throwing a pillow onto the bed. It's way too early to go to bed, but we will drown together if we stay in the kitchen.

"Here, this is for you." I hand her the shirt.

She gives me an appreciative look. Immediately, she begins to pull her shirt up.

"Fuck, Lucy." I quickly cover my eyes and turn around.

"Oh, sorry, I thought you had your bad-idea theory under control, so then this shouldn't be a problem."

I shake my head, and anger begins to boil in me. Partly, because she is so damn determined, and mostly because I want to devour her mouth and take her as if she were mine. "Just be honest with me, you came here tonight to test me."

"No, I came here because I feel somewhat broken and you seem kind of lost, so we can be broken and lost together." Her sincerity is apparent.

Now, I'm not entirely positive she's testing me. She truly believes that we are each other's comfort, and in a way she's right.

I swallow, knowing the best thing I can do in this moment

is wish her good night and leave. Instead, I send us down another spiral, reminding us of last night. "We had our moment, leave it there."

There is no strength left in me to glance over my shoulder and look at her. A deep breath later, and I leave her alone in the room.

Closing my bedroom door behind me, I curse to myself. There are many things that I could do right now to help destress. Play guitar—nope, my songs normally lead me to her. Go for a run—nope, I know I'll return home to her in my bed because she'll want to tease me. Meet up with Knox—nope, the last thing he needs to know is that his little sister is staying at my place.

Throwing my shirt off, I strip down to my briefs then grab my phone from where it fell onto the floor to put it on the charger. Of course, hell is sending me a reminder that I'm screwed, as my screen is flashing a new message from Grayson.

Grayson: Hey, man, Lucy is leaving college. Wasn't a great conversation. I imagine she isn't thrilled with us. If you see her around Bluetop, can you keep an eye on her? I know she enters her own world when she's upset. Sometimes she listens to you more than us. By the way, Brooke made an overload of brownies and they have your name on it. Poker night is coming up, don't forget!

He inserts an emoji of a smiley face dealing cards, which I didn't even know was a thing.

Growling to myself, I turn the phone on to silent then sit on the side of my bed with my feet planted on the ground. Bouncing my knees, I rub my thighs, trying to keep myself in control.

If only I could have last night to do again. I would rewind

and take it back... No, that's not true. I want to experience kissing her on repeat.

No, Drew, she's upset or confused. Now isn't the time to play around with flirtation. But it's not even that, it's our strong connection that is pulling me further under.

The sound of my door cracking open causes me to freeze. I don't need to look up to know that Lucy Blisswood didn't follow the one rule. And subconsciously, I knew she never would.

That's the problem.

I willingly welcomed her in, knowing that this was probably how it would end up.

I want her closer, even if I can't have her.

I feel her in front of me, and my eyes land on her naked thighs, with my shirt doing a half-ass job—literally—of covering her black lace panties.

I drag my eyes up to Lucy standing over me. Her gaze is full of intent and want.

"You're wrong about something," she begins, then plants her hands on my shoulders. Then, in a swift movement, she's sitting on top of me, straddling me, and my body reacts favorably while my mind wrestles with restraint. "What if we're supposed to have more than one moment?"

"Lucy." Fuck, how many times can I say her name tonight with the intention of warning her, but it only ever comes out as a plea?

I feel her press her body tighter against mine, causing her pussy to sit on top of my cock which is painfully hard in a record amount of time. Her breasts push against my naked chest, her scent taking over my senses, and her eyes don't blink as she waits for me to respond.

Then she grabs my hands and guides them to her hips to

ensure I keep her in place. I can't escape, and I'm the one who should be running away.

But maybe she's right, and in this moment, I can have her.

Damn it, I'll always wonder. And that's no good.

Which is exactly why my mouth swoops over her lips to kiss her.

Because I want her, and for tonight, I can believe that we could be everything.

10

DREW

Her sweet murmur vibrates into my mouth as her arms loop around my neck.

I'm not a fool, this is what I wanted the moment I opened the door. I had to attempt some distance, but having Lucy in my arms was the destination I knew she was after, and I let her in.

My arms encircle her middle, pulling her flush to my body. Our mouths slant to try another position, which only makes each angle a better kiss than the last.

She circles her pelvis on top of me, and it sends us on a spiral down a new path for us. One where I'll be damned if I can find an exit, because I'm moving with her in an unknown direction.

Falling back onto the mattress, I take her with me. Her lips shower me with kisses along my jaw and down my neck, Lucy's devouring me, and that's not how this is going to go.

Using my strength, I keep her tight to my body and roll us over until I'm hovering over her. The entire move makes her squeal in delight. It's fucking music to my ears, and her smile is completely infectious because I feel the hint of my own smile appearing on my face.

I love having her underneath me, her hands finding home on my shoulders and her eyes looking into my own with a confident approval. For a moment, I ignore the fact that my cock is pressed against her pussy, with only a thin layer of cloth between us, or that my shirt has crept up to above her waist, causing her body to be on offer.

My shirt looks good on her, which makes me a little sad that it's going to be off her body soon.

"Keep going," she urges.

It snaps my mind into the reality of what is happening. "There's no going back after this."

She tilts her head up to plant a kiss on my inner arm. "Do I look like I would want that? Keep going," she again insists.

I drag my mouth along her collarbone, feeling her body shiver from the sensitivity of my lips delicately tracing a trail on her skin. Or it could be from my hand traveling up her body to feel that she has no bra on, because of course she wouldn't, she came in determined.

Her body squirms beneath me, and I take that as a sign to give her space. Moving my weight, I come to sitting and watch her crawl back on top of me. Ensuring that my eyes are on her—as if I could look away—her hands find the edges of my shirt, and she slowly peels it up her body and over her head. Tossing it the floor, we sit there as I take in the view of her breasts out on display. Two perfect globes with pebbled nipples.

I swipe my hands to move her hair behind her shoulders, but she captures my hands as soon as they finish, bringing them to her breasts.

Our eyes lock, and I tell her the obvious. "You're beautiful." She doesn't say anything, and I feel like she needs to hear it again. "Lucy, you're way too beautiful for the things that I could do to you." Then she blushes and bats her lashes which only makes me fall for her more.

An almost playful sly smirk tugs on her mouth. "Maybe I've been waiting for you to say that."

I peer up at her as I lean in to take a nipple in my mouth, and she watches. Her bottom lip is trapped between her teeth before her head falls back, offering me more.

A soft moan fills my ears as I slide my mouth to her other side. The feeling of her fingertips gliding along my back encourages me to explore her body.

"Lie down," I whisper.

She smiles shyly and obeys. I take my time drinking in the image of her lying in my bed, but I don't get long because she reaches up behind my neck to pull me down for a kiss, stealing my breath in the process.

Lucy's hand roams between us, and the instant she cups my cock, I groan in the back of my throat. Maybe it's realization that she's touching me or simply the fact that her touch is sending me into another world where lust drives us to do everything without thought.

"Wait." I reluctantly break our kiss, and my mouth places a line of kisses down her body, taking extra care around her belly button, that causes her to laugh my name and her fingers to rake through my hair.

"What are you going to do with me?" Lucy's voice is near breathless, but I hear the intrigue in her tone.

My lips journey back up to her mouth, which makes her whimper from the anticipation that I'm causing. With purpose, I lie on my side on a propped elbow while my hand lowers to sneak under the fabric of her panties to slide along her soaking slit.

We both moan out a sound as I explore her pussy. Lucy

because I'm touching her clit, and me because, Christ, she's ready for me.

We both watch as I stroke her, circling her little pearl, and she nuzzles into my neck as her hand comes to hold my wrist.

"Don't stop." Her voice is desperate and heavy.

"Why would I do that?" I playfully counter.

My finger travels inside her, and I feel that she's tight. Her body writhes and responds to my touch, trying to ride the friction from my fingers.

"Lucy, you're going to drive me crazy."

"Welcome to my life."

I can't get enough of her. I bring another finger inside of her, exploring every inch that I can touch, pulling out and spreading her juices around her clit, until I feel her getting close.

"Let go for me," I coax and kiss her forehead.

Her body begins to tremble, and her hand around my cock tightens. Patience leaves me, and the moment she seems to cool down from her orgasm, I'm quick to move and pull down the cotton.

"Not fair," she pouts and grabs the rim of my briefs.

A sly smirk itches to escape my mouth because I like her persistence; that's always been my problem.

It doesn't take long for both of us to be naked in front of one another, taking a few moments to survey our view, admiring each other.

The short interlude provides me ample time to grab a condom from the bedside table, and I rip the wrapper open and wrap up, noticing that Lucy is watching every move.

"Yes?" I arch an eyebrow at her.

"Nothing." She's near bashful. "Well, it's not nothing. I'm looking at your dick and not complaining, but I wasn't sure if I should say anything." She attempts to hide her grin.

We both move to a better position. She opens her legs wide to welcome me, and my dick slides along her pussy to tease us both. I swear, I may already lose my cool, and I'm not even buried deep inside of her yet.

"Last chance. No going back after this. This changes things," I remind her.

Her eyes roll. "Stop saying it and kiss me."

Leaning down, I capture her mouth as her hand reaches between us to guide my length to her. The moment I begin to inch inside of her, I feel her stiffen, and I stop. "You okay?"

She nods gently. "Yeah, just go... slow."

I follow her cues and move in then out, going deeper every time, watching her carefully to ensure she's not in discomfort. Her eyes hood closed, and after a few pumps, she holds me in place, our eyes fixed and her smile reforming.

I move ever so slightly inside of her and we both gasp, as I seem to have hit the perfect spot for her, and I've just entered a whole new realm of pleasure.

She wraps her legs around my waist, drawing me deeper inside of her. My hand comes to cradle her face as she lies beneath me, our eyes never breaking our connection.

"You feel perfect," I tell her softly.

She swallows and breathes in as I dive in deeper with each thrust. "And you're inside of me... finally."

Shaking my head subtly, I interlace our hands against the pillow while my other arm ensures I don't crush her.

Her leg hitches higher, and the new angle heightens sensitivity to my cock, and I can't deny that I'm racing toward an ending too soon.

"Deeper," she requests, and her free hand squeezes my ass cheek.

I respond by purposely moving in a blunt move which causes her to yelp with a smile.

Withdrawing, I sit on my knees and invite her to sit on top of me. Lucy slides onto me with ease, and our arms wrap around one another as I tilt my hips up.

She nips my shoulder as my lips caress the skin on her collarbone. We enjoy touching one another, our mouths fusing and our eyes meeting in recognition. Cautiously, we slow and get lost in one another, a sort of disbelief at the fact we are finally doing this.

I wish I could tell her this changes everything or whisper sweet words, but I wouldn't make promises in a moment like this. Because this is as special as it's going to get, so I'm not going to throw in a lie.

We move and sync our rhythm together until we both can't take it anymore and pick up the pace.

Reaching between us, I touch her to ensure she comes with me over the edge.

And what a fall off the cliff it is.

———

WE BOTH TOOK turns cleaning up in the bathroom, and now I'm returning to my bedroom in boxers to find Lucy lying under the covers, still naked.

I have to pause for a second to take in the view, a perfect sight—not helpful.

Her facial expression is one that I haven't seen on her before, and I study her for a few seconds. "You okay?"

"Why wouldn't I be?" Her eyes seemed hazed, with disbelief perhaps.

"Don't go shy on me now," I say as I lift the cover to slide in underneath. Quickly I roll to my side so that I can look at her.

Now she's examining me. I cock a brow at her. "Yes?"

"Just checking that you're not having an internal freakout about this."

"No, I'm not." I can say that with confidence, maybe because I'm still riding orgasm endorphins, or tonight, I just want to be selfish.

My answer causes her to scoot in my direction and her body molds to my own. I rest my head on the pillow, inviting her to lay her head against my chest, and yup, her hair against my chest is like silk and her fingers drawing circles on my skin feels like she is touching me to make sure it isn't a dream.

"Drew, what happens when we wake up?"

"Shh, Lucy, it's not even morning yet. Hell, it's not even 10pm. Let's just bask in this evening."

"Does evening mean we are going to do it again before midnight or before we fall asleep in the early hours of morning?"

I stroke her hair and breathe out some relaxation, because the thought of going all night has me excited. "Let a man recover a little. Besides, I need you walking normally tomorrow."

She giggles and wiggles against my body, but then calms down and focuses on her fingers drawing lazy designs on my skin. "Just promise me you won't wake up regretting this," she says softly, and I hear the vulnerability.

I kiss the top of her head, with a need overtaking me to reassure her. "I won't."

I leave out the part where I think this is a dangerous move on our part, because now that I've been inside of her, then I'll be damned if any other man gets to touch her. Which is all the more reason I hate that it makes this more complicated. Off-limits and undeserving, all the reasons we can never work.

But right now, I think I might just pretend that we could be possible.

LUCY

If I open my eyes, he'll be there. I keep saying it in my head on repeat.

In the last few seconds since my body woke, I can't bring myself to open my lids. I know I'm in Drew's bed, I know he's lying next to me because I can feel his heat and weight on the mattress. It's just... I'm scared that it could be a dream, and I want to prolong this for as long as I can.

"Lucy." I hear the smile in his thick morning voice. "I know you're awake."

Busted.

Fluttering my eyes open, instantly I'm met with a subtle grin on his face as he lies on his side and looks down at me. Stubble on his chin makes his eyes extra smoldering, and his focus on me feels like his eyes are bluer than normal.

I can't even imagine what I must look like first thing in the morning. My hair is probably a mess, and my eyes probably zombie-like, as I left my mascara on, and my pajamas... wait, I'm still naked.

That thought alone causes me to wake up, and quickly I glance down. To my relief, I find the duvet covering my body, but then my eyes sideline to Drew who's shirtless—the best view.

"Morning," I manage to say with grogginess in my voice.

I stretch slightly before I turn to adjust my body so I can face Drew.

"Good morning." He's staring at my mouth, and it feels promising, except morning breath is a pain.

"How long have you been awake?" I ask curiously.

I've never seen a grown man blush half-naked in bed, but now I'm a witness to it. Drew stretches his fingers out to glide along my arm, causing a sensitive wave to flow through me.

"Long enough. I'm normally up by six every morning." He doesn't blink, nor does his wry smile fade.

I swallow at that realization. "Right, because it's morning." We spent a night together, a whole night lying next to one another, after he was inside of me.

Heat hits my face as I recall what we did twice last night, and my eyes race to find something to look at that isn't him, because I dread what his words may be this morning. Half of me is optimistic, but the other half knows this man has rules in his head.

My eyes shoot to his, and I decide just to be bold. "What are you going to do with me?"

Wow, that was sultrier than I intended, but I am very much satisfied with my confident tone.

His eyes grow slightly wider, but he doesn't answer. Instead, he brings his finger to my lips, tracing them tenderly, and he watches his every move. "I've laid awake, wondering that very question."

"You don't have an answer?"

Drew gently bobs his head side to side. "No. Only that

I'm not going to label what happened or anything else that happens before you walk out that door."

I can tell he is overthinking scenarios, and I don't understand why he can't just go the easy route and let me in. The frustration from it drives me to take charge, and I move to straddle him, which causes him to fall back to lying flat.

I keep the blanket wrapped around me as I look down at him. "What if I walk right back in through the door?" I'm challenging him, with pure serious thought behind it.

He rolls his eyes and brings his hands to my hips, and I can feel his dick flex in this position. "And there is our problem. I know that unless I nail the door shut that you'll come right back. No matter what I say or want to believe, you're persistent."

My lips twist into a smirk. "One of us has to believe that it's possible."

Drew studies me for a second. "What do you think is possible, Lucy? We don't get to ride off into the sunset on Cosmo 2.0, if that's what's in your head."

I playfully slap him at his idea that I daydream like a child. "Don't treat me like a little girl. I'm the woman you just fucked."

Something I just said charges him, and his hands snake behind me to pull me down flat to his body. "I didn't just fuck you. I had you the way we're always supposed to be, at least for *one* night anyway." He begins to stroke my hair, and I'm starting to realize that he really doesn't like the idea of one night but is just too afraid of something else.

"Don't think, Drew," I murmur into his chest.

We lie there for a few minutes, just us, completely tangled together and lost about what to do. For two very different reasons too. He doesn't want to betray his loyalty, and I'm lost for what to do other than keep trying to change his mind.

Lifting my head to look up at him, I kiss his chin and neck. "Do you think I can take a shower? I want to look somewhat normal when I return home."

"A good plan. Yeah, you can use my bathroom. There are towels under the sink."

I give him a stern eye and wait for him to say more. He realizes this and begins to grin. "Something else?"

"Aren't you going to ask if you can join me?"

A low chuckle escapes him. "I don't need to ask, you're in my house."

"So, you'll join me?"

"Why don't you go start the water, and you'll find out," he taunts.

A wide grin stretches on my face, and I hurry out of bed.

———

THE WATER'S RUNNING, and we both let the warmth surround us. We get our hair wet, and he reaches for a bottle of shampoo. Lathering up the soap, he spreads it through his hair and suds land on my arms that he rubs along my skin.

But we stand there, with giddy looks, holding one another. My cheek lands against his chest as his arms wrap around me.

I wonder if this is all I get. "Soaking this moment in?" I ask softly.

"Something like that." His finger hooks under my chin to guide my gaze up to his, and then he leans in to kiss my lips gently.

I take it as my cue to run my hands along his taut body and circle his ass. Gosh, his ass is so damn hard and quite possibly a crime for being nearly perfect. His tongue dips into my mouth, and the mood changes.

The tender moment of before is now transforming into a heated encounter. His lips trail down my neck, stopping to quickly give attention to my pert breasts and nipples that are hard with arousal. But he doesn't play with them for long, as he moves lower and lower until he's on his knees.

His hands land on my inner thighs to coax them wider.

Fuck, he's going to go down on me in the shower. The mere thought causes my hands to plant against the wall to keep my balance. I feel his firm lips drawing a line up my thighs until his warm mouth lands on my pussy. My entire body jolts from surprise, and then I gasp a moan the moment his tongue circles my clit.

"Drew," I breathe out his name, and I comb my fingers through his hair. His eyes peer up at me for some form of approval, and I can only nod like a woman who is desperate for more.

He finds a rhythm and keeps feasting on me. My eyes close as I take in the throbbing feeling from my clit getting worshipped by his tongue.

Admittedly, doing this in a shower, or the fact a man is going down on me like this, is new to me. Sure, I've had an ex try, but it was sloppy and uneventful. This is fucking seeing rainbows, and my body is about to explode from the overload of friction against my clit, with his finger exploring inside of me. Which is why it doesn't take long until I'm trembling, and he holds me firmly in place so I don't fall.

He doesn't let go until my shaking subsides, and he returns to standing with a satisfied look. He cradles my face in his hands. "You taste like sugar, pure sugar."

He kisses me before I can answer, but I'm not sure I could form a clear sentence anyhow.

Pulling away, he flashes me a mischievous look with a wink before he steps half of his body out of the shower to reach for something, and when he's back under the water, I realize what the little square package is.

"You're really enjoying yourself," I laugh. "And I'm not complaining either."

I reach my hand between us to grab his length, and I think I could hold onto him like this all day.

"Have to make these moments count," he warns me, before with one hand, he sheaths himself, and his mouth steals my breath with a kiss.

I don't care if we drown in here, because at least he isn't pulling away.

———

HALF AN HOUR LATER, I'm back in my clothes from yesterday and walk into the kitchen where Drew is pouring coffee into a mug for me, just as waffles pop up from the toaster.

"Wow, I get breakfast before he kicks me out," I joke.

"I didn't say that I was making you breakfast." He grabs a waffle and begins to smother it in butter on a single plate.

I take a seat at the counter and sip on the coffee as I watch him. "Don't try and pretend that waffle isn't for me. You don't have it in you to be the bad guy."

The plate of waffles lands in front of me and he grabs a bottle of syrup from the side. I smile for my win.

"No labels."

My face turns puzzled as I look at him, wondering what his firm two words mean. He seems to be prepping himself for a monologue.

"No labels," I echo back because I realize he means us.

"You have to figure out college, and I have Hudson to deal with."

"Okay. What are you saying?" I'm struggling to digest his words.

He at last looks up from the waffles. "I don't know. But your brothers sure as hell can't know about this."

I gawk at him. "Oh, pity, I was planning on going to them right now to tell them that Drew finally had his way with me." My sarcastic remark isn't appreciated, as I see his eyes flare and his jaw tick in response. "I'm joking," I assure him.

"Lucy, I don't know how to have you around and not want to touch you." He seems slightly agitated.

I bounce my shoulder up and proudly answer, "You can touch me."

Drew walks around the island and sits on a stool next to me, taking my hands in his. "No plans or questions about what this is." His tone is serious, and I grasp his words.

"This isn't a regret-and-mistake convo?"

"Lucy," he hisses. "You could never be a regret or mistake, you know that. But this is complicated."

"It is if you don't tell me if I can or can't see you again," I reply, as I need clarity.

A grin forms on his mouth, and he seems to ease. "No matter what I say, you'll see me again. You'd make sure of that. Fucking stubborn you are."

"Yes, but will you kiss me again?" I pry for more details.

"A fair chance that I might. Doesn't mean I should. In fact, what happened in the last forty-eight hours really should be a one-time thing." He seems humorously defeated.

I crawl my fingers up his arm like a spider.

"I'm going to hell," he groans.

I tip my head back and look at him. "Nah, you're going to heaven since you deserve all the good things. Just so happens that I'm one of those items." I nuzzle his nose with my own, which seems to catch him off guard. May be a little too cutesy for him.

Bouncing off my chair, I grab my purse from the side. "Would love to stay, but I need to head back before a search party comes looking."

Drew settles into the chair with his arms hanging on the back. "Lucy, just remember that not everything ends up the way we want it."

I stop for a moment to think about his remark. "Only if you don't take chances." I give him a reassuring smile and turn to leave.

I know full well that my heart is taking a chance on him, but is it a chance? My heart already belongs to him. He already had it since the moment I sat in his truck all those years ago.

12

LUCY

Walking into Grayson's house, it's painfully silent. It shouldn't be this way, not on a Saturday at least. There should be Rosie yelling that she wants something, Brooke calling back to use manners, all while Bella giggles, oblivious to the chaos.

I stop in my tracks when I enter the kitchen. Brooke and Grayson are sitting side by side at the island, attacking a plate of brownies.

"Afternoon, as it is no longer morning," Grayson greets me, and Brooke touches his arm, almost trying to calm him.

"Hey Lucy, want a brownie?" She smiles warmly.

Taking a spot near the kitchen sink, I hop up to sit on the counter. "Okay, lay it on me."

Grayson leans back on the stool. "It's fine, you were at Kendall's, I know, and you're not a teenager anymore."

Rolling my eyes. "And? I know a but is coming." I have a stare-off with my oldest brother.

"He's just concerned." Brooke looks at Grayson, then me, then back to Grayson. "And he thought maybe we should all talk while the girls are at Bennett's."

Puffing out a breath, I remind myself that I knew this was coming. "Fine."

"I don't think you should jump to decisions now. Take a week or two to look at your options. But if you really don't want to finish college then… you know the drill." Grayson is reminding me that I'll need to get a job.

I roll a shoulder and adjust my neck. "It's a work in progress, but I may have a solution to my financial resources."

His eyes grow big. "What the hell does that mean?"

"Don't worry, big brother." I pick a grape off the fruit bowl to examine.

Brooke clears her throat and seems to kick Grayson under the counter.

"Okay, moving on. And where will you stay?" he asks.

Admittedly, that is a bit tricky, and I feel my face fall into a frown. "I need to… I need a little time to figure it out."

"Well, you know you can stay here," Brooke offers.

"I'm not going to kick you to the curb," Grayson says. "The girls love having you here. Plus, when the little boy comes, extra hands will be appreciated."

Brooke pinches Grayson's arm with a playful grin. "Hey, it could be a girl."

He flashes her an affectionate look before his laser eyes return to me. "It just means no sleepovers."

I nearly fall off the counter but save myself just in time. "Oh?" My voice hitches slightly. "Why would you say that?"

Grayson grabs another brownie, because although in shape, brownies are his downfall. "I don't know. I mean, I hear Sean is back in Bluetop for the summer. You two had a thing in high school, no?"

"We went to prom together as friends, hardly constitutes something worth rekindling," I volley back.

Brooke laughs softly as she grabs hold of her mug of tea. "I think what your brother is trying to say is if you're living here, then no fooling around, well, not in the guest room or anywhere within the property line."

My palm flies up to stop them both. "Clear. Topic closed."

Grayson shakes his head, clearly done with this conversation too. "Okay, well, good chat, everyone." He gives a little fist pump in the air. "I'm going to go mow the grass."

"We have one of those robot mower things," Brooke reminds him.

He kisses Brooke's cheek. "Right." Grayson disappears anyway.

Brooke and I look at one another with a funny look, almost as if she can see into my soul.

Calmly she drinks from her tea. "Hey, I was thinking we should have a ladies' night. Kelsey, Madison, you, and me. Eighteen and over, so no Rosie."

I grab a banana. "Because you really want a night off or because everyone is freaking out, when I am totally fine."

Brooke leans back in the chair. "I know you're fine. In fact, you look kind of elated. Have a good night?"

I busy myself with the banana to avoid her looking me straight in the eye. "Yep." It comes out too easy, and my voice sounds strange.

"Good... And it's for me. I think all of us ladies could do with a night. It's been ages since we've had you here to join us. We could go for dinner or for drinks at Rooster Sin, maybe we can watch Drew play."

"Drew?" I croak out, but when I look at her, I see that she innocently made the suggestion, but my body already feels like it wants to scream inside that maybe he's mine, since we have a deeper connection now.

Brooke continues, "Yeah, or maybe we can all go shopping."

"You know, just a simple night doing nails and snacks sounds perfect," I reply with a smile as I leave.

"Okay, I'll arrange something," she calls back.

The moment I close the bedroom door behind me, I hop onto the bed like a jellyfish with an elated sigh.

My body feels thoroughly touched, and I close my eyes to remember Drew's mouth all over my skin. For the entire night, I could just feel safe and grounded, alive and certain. His arms around me have a positive effect, even when the world around me feels like it's rocking.

Then I return here, and even though I hate lying to Brooke and my brother, it's not exactly a lie. Delaying information perhaps, but is it? I guess if Drew decides there's nothing more between us, then nobody will ever know.

I don't think long about that, and roll to my side, as I need a few minutes to just lie still. The smell of the fabric softener hits my nose, and I sniff it again. It reminds me of my senior year of high school when we moved in with Brooke. She always takes care of the tiny things, laundry being one, and it's nice having someone who wants to dote on you the way a mother or older sister would. Just like, I bask in the thought of going into the kitchen, knowing the fridge is stocked, or that a little child may come at me with a giant hug at any moment.

It's all the things that I didn't have when I was hours deep into research papers and essays. I guess it was good old-fashioned homesickness as one of the many reasons to send me back here.

And now I have no reason to ever leave. Because Drew kissed me, then last night we spent it together the way I've only dreamed about.

Even when I look at my phone to check my inbox, I still can't wipe this smile away, even when I still have no new emails. Because it doesn't matter. I'll find a way to make everything work out.

———

"WINE?" Kelsey asks me, with her eyes giving me a pointed look. It's already been established that Brooke can't drink, for obvious reasons, Madison seems to want an alcohol-free night, which means Kelsey needs a partner in crime, and that leaves me.

We're hanging out at Kelsey and Bennett's house. It used to be the house where I lived with my father for a few years before he passed. They've now made it their own.

"Sure, can't exactly say no to the family brand," I tell her as I take a seat around the dining table that holds enough snacks to feed an army, plus a row of nail polish colors.

Growing up, I was surrounded by my brothers, and we aren't even close in age. But Brooke kind of took me under her wing when she used to be our neighbor, then Kelsey too when Brooke and Grayson got back together. Naturally, they welcomed Madison into the family when that time came.

"How was the other night? Brooke mentioned you had a night out with Kendall?" Kelsey slides a glass in my direction.

My mind recalls the story I rehearsed. "Fine. Just a movie, dinner, then spent the night. We stayed up quite late, so slept in."

"On Friday?" Madison, who is creating a cheese-and-cracker sandwich, seems to be curious.

"Yep." I quickly drink from my wine.

Brooke grabs a nail polish, a peachy pink. "I wonder how

the guys are doing with poker night at our place." All my brothers and Drew are playing poker at Grayson's house. They were supposed to the other day, but they changed the night.

"Hey, Lucy, I forgot about the ice cream in the freezer in the garage. Do you mind helping me?" Kelsey's question seems out of nowhere, and probably isn't true. She's always been a horrible liar, but I play along.

"Sure."

Soon enough, we're both away from the group, inside the garage, and not heading in the direction of her freezer.

She touches my arm to guide my attention to her. "Spill it."

"Huh? You tell me, where's the ice cream?" I look in the direction of the fridge, trying my best to play along.

Kelsey's hand comes to her hip. "You weren't with Kendall." The garage light highlights her serious look.

"What do you mean?"

"I was working at the salon Saturday morning bright and early." Her finger comes up to her chin. "Funny, guess who I saw." I swallow and realize this isn't going to go in my favor. "Yep, Kendall, with her mom, because she wanted to get her hair done before leaving town."

I throw on a fake smile. "Oh, funny."

Kelsey shakes her head and grins. "Just know that if you're doing whatever with whoever, and I can only guess, then come up with a better story and fact check."

Her tone and body language is a relief, and I actually appreciate that someone is somewhat aware of the best night of my life.

"You're going to tell Bennett?"

She snickers. "Lucy, have you seen your nephews? Most days I'm surprised if I even remember to double moisturize my face." Such a Kelsey thing to say. Even with two rambunctious boys running around, she always looks like she stepped out of a photoshoot. "Besides, I don't want to set off Bennett. He can turn into a bit of bull when it comes to you and boys. Then again, nothing compared to Grayson and Knox." She laughs to herself and pats my shoulder.

"Right." There is zero excitement in my voice.

Kelsey walks me back into the house, and soon we are at the table with everyone chatting, polishing nails, and drinking our chosen beverages.

While Brooke and Kelsey talk about planning a trip to the zoo, Madison and I focus on our nails.

"I'm sorry," I whisper.

Madison quickly looks up from the brush with baby-blue polish on her nail, then back. "For what?"

I bite my inner cheek, aware that I won't feel better until I've cleared the air. "Leaving college." After all, she was my high school guidance counselor and wrote my recommendations before marrying my brother.

Quickly, she puts the brush back in the bottle and slides it away. All of her attention moves to me, and her arm comes around me to pull me into a side hug. "Now isn't the time to get into details. You must have your reasons, and even though I think you should look into a few options to finish your degree, tonight is just… relax night." An assuring smile forms on her mouth. "Everyone deserves a little time to just be free in the moment, and if you feel so inclined, then you can share the details of the other night." Her voice and eyes grow coy.

My eyebrows raise as I play with the cap of my purple polish.

Madison giggles slightly then leans in to speak low. "Lucy, remember, before we were family, I was your teacher.

And I'm on to your using Kendall as an excuse." She touches the top of my hand. "I hope everything works out the way you've dreamed." She winks then returns to join the conversation happening on the other side of the table.

I smile to myself as I look around the room, realizing how lucky I am to have such an amazing tribe of women who will be there when I scream to the universe that everything will be alright or quite possibly when my world crumbles.

I'm more than certain that I made the right decision coming back to Bluetop.

———

RETURNING TO GRAYSON'S HOUSE, Brooke pulls us up in the driveway just as my brothers and Drew are all wrapping up their own evening.

I haven't seen Drew since the other morning, and the moment I get out of the car and our eyes land on one another, I think I may melt.

And now I wonder what he'll do, because my brothers are around. But this is the first time that we're being thrown into this situation since our own dynamic has changed. Even in the darkness with the light from above the garage on, I can see Drew's watching me with an intense stare that I swear may be part werewolf or just pure territorial claim now that he's touched me, and it's replaying in his head in this very moment.

Then I notice that everyone is staring at us. And suddenly I feel like they may be on to us.

13

DREW

I wasn't expecting that seeing her again would cause me to want to grab her and kiss her with an urge almost impossible to ignore.

I knew running into her again was inevitable, but why does it have to be now when her entire family is watching, totally oblivious to what's shifted between us?

Brooke quickly says good night to everyone before disappearing inside, and then I have all three Blisswood brothers looking at Lucy and me with a sort of awkwardness.

"Who won?" Lucy asks, crossing her arms as we all stand in a circle.

Bennett slaps a hand on Knox's shoulder. "This one here swept us under the table, as always."

"Talent is talent." Knox brings his car key into the air then indicates that he is going to leave. "I'm off, boys."

Good, now we're down to only two spectators. I can't help but notice that Bennett has this sort of wry almost-sure smile. It's faint, but I make no mistake that it's there. "I'll head out too."

Grayson scratches his cheek. "You two kids don't stay too

long out here. Lucy, can you turn the security system on when you head back in?"

"Sure," she replies.

Grayson stares directly at me with a sort of firmness that should make me nervous, but it doesn't.

And then Lucy and I are alone.

Two people standing and studying one another.

"They want you to talk to me, to make sure that I'm okay, huh?" A knowing smirk forms on her mouth.

I bring my hands behind my head to stretch my body. She isn't far off, but it feels like something else that I can't quite pinpoint. "Maybe. It did come up during poker, but I'm not going to say anything to you that you don't already know."

She steps closer, and I send a reminder to my feet to stay firm. My body stands taller and at attention, but I already feel a weakening in my soul.

"Anything else you talked about?" she rasps.

Keep it together, Drew.

"Not about you, no," I answer honestly. In truth, it was a little easy to hang out with her brothers. It was the usual talk of sports, music, and life. For a few hours, it felt like nothing had happened to change that dynamic. Probably because Lucy wasn't around to remind me of how I had her moaning underneath me.

"Of course not." She reaches out her finger to tap my arm. "I guess I should probably go inside, take a shower, lie in bed, think of things."

Swallowing, I can't get the image out of my head. Will she touch herself? I bet she will.

"That's... a... good... plan." My words are a struggle, and I feel my conscience letting go, especially when she steps even closer.

"Why? Because it's away from you or because I'll be

thinking of you?" Her sight lands on my mouth, and I lick my lips. Damn those new outside lights that Grayson installed a few months back, I can see the outline of her face.

This time I step forward, my eyes quickly scanning the scene, and when I see we're alone, I grab hold of her hips to lead her around my truck. Even more hidden and against my car is the safest option right now. Except it isn't safe at all.

With only a breath's distance between us, I feel heat spread against my skin. "Lucy, you're going to be my undoing." I can't help it and lean in to trace the outline of her jaw with the tip of my nose.

"Is this how it's going to go every time I see you?" she whispers as she tries to capture my mouth with her own.

I laugh bitterly to myself, deep in my throat. I feel the humor in that question, and it could make me want to laugh for years. "This isn't how this should be going at all. I need to stay away from you, but since you've been back, I can't control anything." I step back, and my fingers come up to rub my temples.

"Hmm, that's going to be hard." I love the sound of her hums.

Looking up at the sky, I give up.

My hand reaches out to glide along her cheek until I have a firm hold, cradling her face. Stepping forward, I plant my lips on her own. Without question she kisses me back, because she's been waiting for me to snap, and it didn't take long.

If we weren't standing in the driveway of her brother's house, I swear I would punish her for testing me.

Her hands grip my t-shirt as she gives everything to me through her breath and kiss. She tastes like chocolate and wine tonight, and who doesn't love that combination?

Another firm kiss, then I break away from her spell.

Undeniably, I know I have a grin on my face. "This can't be how this goes."

"You know Grayson has a security camera above the garage that he's probably watching from." Her one-toned declaration has my head whipping in the direction of the garage, but then she immediately giggles, and I look back at her. "You're too easy. Relax."

I shake my head and move closer to keep her body trapped between my car and myself. "I need you to go inside ASAP, do that for me?"

"Sure. Grayson mentioned something the other day about how I should give Sean from prom another chance, so I should probably give him a call anyway." She's playing with me, yet I can't help this feeling of a claim that I want to make on her.

"Fuck that." I lean in to quickly nip her neck, but not enough to leave a mark—unfortunately. "You're not even interested. Do you know how I know?"

"Tell me," she challenges.

I drag my thumb along her bottom lip. "Because you may have gone on one date with him way back, but even then, you were thinking of me. Haven't you always? This thing between us, it isn't new. We're stuck in one another's heads, always have been."

Her face goes still, her eyes don't blink, instead, she gently nods in agreement before a smile spreads.

We both stand there, aware that we can't find an out from one another, not yet. This will only keep happening, so we might as well acknowledge that we're stuck together.

Lucy clears her throat and looks away. "I guess this means I should bring you lunch or wait for you after work."

"Don't you fucking do it." I can't control this smile on my

face or my eyes as I pretend to be annoyed, because I know she won't listen.

She pats my cheek. "I wouldn't dare." She pretends to pout. "Good night." Lucy leans up on her toes to kiss me on the corner of my mouth.

This is going to spiral, I know it.

———

LEANING over the table in the barn, I look at Grayson's blueprints as some of the crew saw pieces of wood. Olive Owl is getting another expansion, this time a small building that will be Kelsey's spa. I guess wine and spas go hand in hand, and they've talked about it for years.

Grayson throws a pencil. "The delivery for more wood is delayed."

"That's not a problem, we can just go ahead and lay cement for this corner room." I point onto the paper.

"You're going to put us ahead of schedule again," he muses.

Scratching the back of my neck, I try to suppress my pride as I notice Grayson look behind me, and quickly I turn.

No fucking way.

She really wants to send me under.

Lucy is walking toward us with a bright smile, a ponytail that sways with her stride, a short, light green summer dress that leaves little to the imagination, and she's carrying a small cooler. "Thought I would bring lunch to my favorite people."

I must be standing there with a dumbfounded look, while Grayson is happy as a clam and reaches out to grab the lunch supplies. "Wow, lucky us. Did you make this or did my wife play a role?"

Lucy pretends to be offended. "All me, thank you very

much. By the way, Brooke wanted me to remind you to pick up Rosie from her summer ballet camp. It finishes at 2."

Grayson grabs a foil-wrapped sandwich and looks at his watch. "Yikes, I need to get moving then. I'll be back after. Hold down the fort, okay." He points to me before heading off without a thought.

I look at Lucy as I lean against the table, completely onto her tricks. "Let me guess, you timed it so he would leave us?"

"Guilty. Now, is it your lunch break or not?" She looks around to see that nobody is taking much notice of us.

What the hell, here I go again.

"Come on, let's go find some shade," I suggest.

Ten minutes later, we're sitting under a tree near the Olive Owl property line, and there's enough shade to keep us cool on this scorching day.

I now fully examine the contents of the cooler. "Really going for persuasion, huh?" I raise my brows at her when I spot a bottle of ranch dressing and a Tupperware filled with cut veggies.

"I think I've come to learn that you have no spine when it comes to me. No persuasion needed. Instead, I just wanted to bring your favorites." She leans back on her arms with a water bottle in one hand.

I take one of the foiled chicken wraps she made and get comfortable next to her.

"Keeping busy other than being a pain in my ass?" I ask her, as I wonder what she's up to during the day since she doesn't have a job, nor is she studying.

She wobbles her head in consideration. "I slept in, and truthfully it felt so good to just... sleep. Waking and knowing I'm not rushed to finish a paper or need to focus on a to-do list is what I needed." Lucy explains it so simply, but I hear the sincerity.

For the first time since she's been back, I realize that her words haven't been just that. She's exhausted, and rest is something she's after.

"Taking it easy, huh?"

"Probably sounds silly to you. Anyway, I helped Brooke with Bella then went to see Kelsey to take the boys to the park for a little bit, and now here I am." Her hand lands on my arm, and she purposely looks at my bicep before squeezing.

I don't brush her off, instead let her keep her touch on me as I take a bite from the wrap. "Not bad." I indicate to the sandwich, but truthfully this is fucking fantastic, with the portion of chicken and mayo just right.

"Good," she chirps out as she interlinks our arms. We both look out straight ahead into the open field and taking in the sound of a breeze.

I'm not one to recognize many emotions, but at this very moment, I can tell that, although happy, Lucy has things on her mind, and not necessarily me either. "You okay?"

She side-glances at me and realizes that I've been studying her. Her mouth parts open slightly, and she hesitates, but then continues. "It's fine. I'm just really content to be sitting here, and even though I need to give some answers to my brothers about my next steps, I feel at peace. That's possible, right?"

"Very possible."

She rests her head on my shoulder as she sighs, more a relaxation breath than anything. "Did you write any more songs about me?"

A whole fucking book. "You'll just have to listen one day to figure it out."

"I think I skipped the whole part where I should have told

you that it was a beautiful song and you really are talented, but we kind of got occupied," she mentions.

I snort a laugh because her reasoning is the best way to explain it. "Thanks."

"Want to know a secret?"

"If it involves you."

"I wrote a novel."

My forehead forms lines. "What do you mean?"

"I wrote a book, and if all goes well, then it'll be published."

I'm impressed, though I'm not surprised. She's capable of anything, especially writing, as that was always her favorite subject. "What kind of book?"

She laughs to herself. "One that I would hope my brothers never read."

My eyes dart to her. She has a nervous smile, and then I wonder if my mind is connecting the dots correctly. "As in one of *those* books?" I tip my nose down and try to hide my amusement.

Lucy pinches my arm. "Something like that."

"Okay, tell me I'm not market research," I joke.

"Nah, well, not really. I already wrote the book months ago, now I'm just waiting to see what will come of it."

I finish the wrap and then move to lean on my side to look at Lucy. "Is that your plan B?"

She shrugs a shoulder. "Hopefully."

"Are you sure Bluetop is your final destination?" I wonder, because when she went off to college, she was excited to go away, be her own person, and have opportunities that she may not find in Bluetop.

Lucy gives me a peculiar look. "Dreams change, and every day back feels more like I never should have left."

My fingers circle patterns around her knee, and I watch

them. "You should have left, and you did. Now you have perspective."

She hooks her fingers under to capture my own until we're holding hands like two people meant to interact this way. "Exactly. I can focus on starting a new chapter in my life."

I can't drag my eyes away from our hands entwined; it's odd, yet right. "You mean adulthood?" I quip.

She shoots me a warning glare. "But anyways, enough about that. Any Hudson news?"

Of course she would ask, she's curious and cares.

"I'm going to see him next week. We're meeting halfway, need to find somewhere. I mean, he's given so many options. I could have met him at his home, but I don't know, I feel like our first meeting should be somewhere neutral."

"Neutral is perfect. Do you have any idea about halfway points?"

I shake my head no. "Truthfully, I feel a bit out of my depth about how to approach this."

Lucy brings her hand to rest on my shoulder as she lies on her side next to me. "A goat farm." We both laugh at her ridiculous suggestion. "Don't be nervous. And don't over-think it. At the very least you can say that you share the same DNA as Hudson Arrows."

A shaky hum vibrates in my mouth. I wish I had her confidence on the matter.

"I'll wait for you when you come back. Will that ease your stress?" she offers with a mischievous grin, yet there's sincerity hiding behind it.

"Not in the slightest." I keep my demeanor simple. "Well, I should probably head back."

"You're not going to kiss me?" She seems surprised.

A devilish grin crawls on my lips, I feel it. "No, not here.

First, I wouldn't just kiss you. Not when you're wearing a dress that would make it so easy for my fingers to slide under and confirm how wet you are. And two, your brother is about to descend upon us." I indicate with my head off into the distance.

"Grayson went to get Rosie," Lucy objects.

I let go of her hand and pat her leg. "Yeah, and you have two other brothers who all work out on a daily basis and may kill me." I stand up and wipe my hands on my jeans, nodding my head to Knox who is approaching us.

Lucy quickly bounces up when she too notices her brother.

"I heard a rumor my sister brought lunch yet forgot to bring me mine." Knox drags his sunglasses to his head to give Lucy a pointed stare. "Good spot, it's a little brutal out today. I was just checking on the grapes in the fields, and I think I'm going to need to set an extra sprinkler session."

"Probably a good idea." I scratch my cheek, trying to avoid any indication that this is an unusual circumstance; in fact, it's becoming quite *usual*.

"Want to go for a run later?" Knox asks, because running in summer heat only revs us up to push more.

"Maybe tomorrow, I kind of want to finish some things with the construction when Grayson gets back," I explain.

Knox turns his attention to Lucy who is picking up the cooler. "What's up with you? Making plans for the summer?"

"Is that a general question or a reminding-me-to-get-my-shit-together kind of question?" She rolls her eyes and slams the cooler into Knox's arms. "Here. Your timing sucks. Have the leftovers." She then walks off.

Knox looks at me with his eyes wide, and he puffs out a breath. "She's a little touchy."

I can only imagine why. She's either pissed I didn't kiss

her or annoyed that I don't want her brothers to know. Then the cherry on top is Knox reminding her of what she's trying to take a rest from—life.

"Just let her be. I think she needs to kind of unwind for a few weeks, maybe she was a little too stressed." It's my attempt to plant a seed in his head.

"Yeah, maybe. Thanks again for always being there for her."

"Of course. Uhm, I should get back."

The twist in my stomach feels like a knife that Knox has no clue he's holding. Escape is the best option.

———

THE NEXT FEW DAYS, I focus on the grind of work. I make my days longer than normal because I'm trying not to think about Lucy or Hudson. I'm sitting on my porch with my guitar after work and play around with a few chords, drinking from a cold bottle of beer occasionally.

I notice Lucy drive up to the curb in her car. I stay put because yet again she shows up unexpectedly. Quickly she slides out of her seat and nearly skips up the front sidewalk wearing too-short shorts and a tank top, until she's standing in front of me.

"I don't have long. I've been sent on an errand," she states.

"Okay, and?"

She smiles wide before she nearly jumps forward, leans down, captures my face with her hands, and kisses me hard into next year. She has a point to prove. I almost drop my guitar but balance myself by just letting her have her way with me.

Pulling back, she rubs my lips with her thumb. "You

owed me a kiss from the other day. And I just wanted to tell you that I'll be waiting for you right here, whether you like it or not, after you see Hudson. You've got this."

"Okay." I have to say that I really like her assurance right now.

She gives me one more smile before she turns and bounces out of my night.

For the first time in weeks, I feel like meeting my biological father may just go all right.

14

DREW

My eyes scan the patio of the restaurant as I follow the hostess. It's a decent halfway point between simple and a little too chic, but it seemed like the easiest meeting place, as Hudson drove out from the city and I came from Bluetop.

It's another warm summer day, with a breeze that makes it pleasant outside. We're nowhere noticeable on a map, but the restaurant looks over a man-made pond. It seems there must be a golf course nearby, as the majority of people sitting sipping from their glass filled with iced tea and slices of lemon are wearing golf attire.

I can feel that my hands want to move from nerves, but that's been the whole drive here. It was impossible to stay focused, but a blaze of curiosity gave me enough adrenaline to keep going.

Meeting my dad.

Yep, just a normal weekend.

It must be an unfair disadvantage for Hudson. I can read everything about him online: his career playing football before he started coaching as one of the league's youngest coaches, what charities he contributes to, and how he's living a bachelor's life with millions in the bank. I must be a blank slate to him, with not much to find online anyways.

The hostess leads me around a corner, and there's a private patio with only one table. My heart admittedly quickens, as Hudson is already sitting there. Dark jeans, a dark green t-shirt with sunglasses tucked in the collar. His hair is the same shade as my own, and eyes blue as the sea and all too familiar. Since I've received the news that he's my father, I've secretly hoped that I have his genes. The man may be pushing forty, but he looks well under.

He quickly stands up with a hesitant smile or maybe he's unsure what to do.

"Thank you. Do you mind leaving us alone for a little bit before returning to take our order?" he requests of the hostess. I vaguely hear, "Yes, Mr. Arrows."

"Hi." His attention on me is odd because his awkwardness is identical to my own.

"Hi," I reply.

We both step forward, and he offers me his hand to shake, then seems to question if that was the right move. "Sorry. Is this how you do this? I mean, I don't exactly have practice in meeting my adult son, and I'm not sure about the protocol."

I like that he's honest about it, and I shake his hand to be polite. "It's… okay. I mean, not sure there's a rule book for this."

He offers me a half-smile. "Please, sit down. I ordered a pitcher of iced tea and two beers, figured we should keep our options open." His arm indicates to go sit at the table.

We both assess one another as we slowly sit down. I wonder if I'm what he imagined or if he's already disappointed.

"It's good to finally meet you. I've been a nervous wreck since I found out," he admits.

I appreciate his candor. "I would be worried if this was an average day at the office for you," I retort. I take a deep breath, wondering where to start. "It's nice here. Why did you suggest this place?"

Hudson takes a sip from his beer bottle. "I stop by sometimes on my way to my lake house. We're busy preparing for the new season but have a few days off for summer break. I'm in the city during the week and try to come out on weekends or holidays. They do a really good steak here."

I'm unable to relate to anything from his sentence, except steak. Humans always turn to food as a safe conversation topic. "Steak sounds good."

"The ride up okay? I've heard Bluetop is worth a visit. I was invited once to a wedding at Olive Owl but couldn't go due to a schedule conflict. A restaurant owner I know got married there."

I scratch at my ear with the back of my thumb. "Really? Or did your investigator look into Bluetop?" Very quickly I realize that all came out wrong. "Sorry. I didn't mean to, well, I don't know…"

He leans over the table with his eyes set on me. "It's okay, this is an unusual circumstance. Really, I was supposed to go to a wedding. Back then I had no clue I even had a son. I found out when Cecily, your mother's old friend from high school, reached out. I didn't believe her at first, admittedly."

I take a gulp from my beer. "I can imagine."

Hudson sighs and sinks back against his chair. "You have no contact with Tara, your mom? I… don't remember her so much, it was a summer-party kind of thing."

I laugh. "Not since she walked out when I was just a kid."

"I'm sorry. And your da—"

"Keith. That's who raised me, and don't worry, he doesn't win any father-of-the-year awards, so you don't need to owe him a debt of gratitude." Talking about this makes a form of resentment stir inside of me. I knew this topic would come up, but it still sucks to remind everyone of the situation.

Hudson glances away then back to me. "I'm going to be honest. I know most of what you're going to say. The benefit of having money is paying someone to look into things, but I want to hear it from you. I need to know that you're okay." His tone is nearly somber.

I brush off his concern. "Why wouldn't I be? I have a job, a house, and friends."

"I just wish… it would have gone differently for you."

"Don't feel sorry for me." There's an edge in my tone.

A hint of a smirk forms on his mouth. "You remind me of myself. Must be genetic."

"You only just met me."

His smirk stretches. "It's your offense that your body and words give off, it's me at your age."

"Look, Hudson, I really don't know what you want from me. You're not at fault for being in the dark, and I'm a grown man now. We can scratch off my childhood as a total miss, that's just life." I take another drink from my beer.

"Okay, then let's focus on now. I like your tattoo." He indicates with his head to my arm. "I also have a couple, one on my back and one on my upper arm. Getting one kind of goes with football life. Now I'm tied to wind breaker jackets during games, so nobody really notices."

I touch my arm out of instinct. "Got it when I was eighteen, ironic that it's an arrow."

He tips his bottle of beer at me. "Life is always playing with us. What else? Hobbies? Are you a football fan? I can get you box seats, you should come to a game." He seems excited at the prospect.

"I don't really watch it, although it's a good sport. I wrestled in high school, now I box with a friend."

"Oh yeah? Do you compete?"

"No," I answer.

Hudson's face falls. "Hobbies?"

"I play guitar, write some music too."

"Yeah? Do you have a concert coming up? Working on an album?"

I snicker again. "Nope. Just a few performances at the local bar. Nothing professional." I feel like I'm failing at all his questions, being one dissatisfaction after another to him.

"That sounds cool. I mean, I'm not really a musical person, that must be from your mom's side."

A silence overtakes us, probably because he mentioned my mom again. The thorn in both of our sides, the reason that we're sitting here now as two adults trying to find a connection.

"Work?" Hudson tries again.

I glance around to see that the staff really are leaving us alone, as there's nobody in sight. "I work construction, help out at Olive Owl. You probably know these answers, so let me spell it out for you. I'm happy with it; I don't feel like I'm climbing some ladder or that I'm unsatisfied. Grayson treats me well, and I was able to save up enough money for a house." I scoff. "Man, if you'd met me five years ago, then it probably would've been a different situation. But you don't need to go home trying to figure out how to make it up to me that I was dealt a shitty hand of cards then, because I'm fine now."

Hudson looks at me with an almost entertained yet panicked look, with his hands coming up to indicate for me to stop. "I'm sorry. I'm doing this all wrong. I have no fucking clue what to ask or say. I didn't even know I had a son until a few months ago, and not even just that, but a son I can have a beer with."

Damn it, I'm being an ass. I should probably loosen a notch or something, as this guy is genuinely trying to get to know me, and I'm not even sure he's judging me. It just feels like people are always forming an opinion, and I wish I had more to be proud of.

The waitress comes to our table, clearly unaware that she's walking in on the awkward-as-fuck moment between two grown men.

"Would you two like to order something to eat? Asparagus is the vegetable of the day." The woman my age smiles.

Hudson looks between the waitress and myself. "I think… hope… we're staying for lunch."

If I wasn't driving, I would ask for something stronger right now. "Yeah, steak is fine."

Relief hits Hudson's face, and he orders the same.

When the waitress is out of sight, the air of thick tension continues.

"Listen, you set the tone for our relationship moving forward. Maybe this is it for us, but I sure as hell hope not. I would love to get to know you more and invite you to my lake house or for a stay in the city. April would love to meet you, I'm sure."

I cut in. "April?"

He scratches the back of his neck and smiles. "Yeah. She's around your age." He quickly flies his palm up to stop any of my theories from forming. "No, I wasn't completely reckless with birth control when I was younger. April is my goddaughter and niece, she's my older sister's daughter." He waves a hand to end the explanation.

"Oh. Do you have a big family?" Now my curiosity about his world is piqued.

Hudson relaxes again, this time grabbing a peanut from the bowl of nuts that I didn't notice. "Not really. Just my parents and sister. My parents will probably go through the roof when they hear I have a son, and in a good way." He looks at me and must feel like he said something wrong. "I've wanted to tell them, but I wasn't sure what you would want."

I give him one nod in understanding. "And according to the internet, no girlfriends or wives at this moment... or this week anyway."

He grins, clearly appreciating the humor of my comment. "Drew, I'm still young. You?"

My jaw flexes as I think about that. I don't have a girlfriend, per se, I have a Lucy. The woman who I seem to be starting something that resembles a relationship with, even though I shouldn't. Yet, is it new? Because she's been in my life for a long time. "There isn't exactly a girlfriend." I gulp.

Hudson leans over and touches my arm. "I feel like there's more to it, but I'm in no position to press on." He grabs his sunglasses from his shirt and places them back over his eyes. "Tell me more about your craftsmanship projects. Any more bookshelves?"

Confusion hits me, and my face must look puzzled. "How do you know about that?" I doubt his investigator is that thorough.

Hudson pauses as if he's been caught out. "The bookcase... it's in my dining room at the lake house."

It registers to me that the bookshelf I sold a few months ago, I sold it to someone who purchases furniture for their store in the city, they've never been to Bluetop. I didn't know who received the piece of furniture in the end. "It was you."

"Guilty."

Now I feel anger, mostly because for a moment I felt I had talent and someone wanted to buy my piece of work. Instead, they bought it because of pity or wanting to somehow get to know me. I shake my head, annoyed, and stand. "You know, this was probably a bad idea."

Hudson stands too. "Wait, did I do something wrong? Fuck, of course I did. I sent someone to buy your shelf when I was trying to figure out if you were my son." Now he just seems to be talking to himself until he looks up at me. "Really, it's true that I wanted a piece of you in my house. Which right now sounds kind of creepy, but I assure you that it's a fucking beautiful piece of work. Everyone always asks about it when I have people over, and they beg me to give the contact details of who created it so they can order one. But I don't because what am I supposed to say? 'Sure, Drew, my son who I haven't yet met made it.'"

"People want to order my bookcase?" A trickle of a feeling that I've done something right hits me.

"Yes! Like five people have asked. I haven't even had the pre-season party at my place, and then I'm sure you'll get five more people." He's eager to assure me. Is it a father thing or a Hudson thing?

I step back closer to the chair and slide my hands along my jeans. "I'm sorry. I just… I'm used to being on my own." Hudson looks at me but says nothing. I sit down again and so does he.

"I get it. This is fucking weird. But I think we're doing okay considering we don't have any whiskey. Hell, even a joint at this rate is looking alright." He sounds defeated.

I have to smile at his comment.

The waitress returns with our food, and when Hudson asks if she can bring a bowl of ranch dressing, I have a feeling that this may not be too bad.

———

OVER THE NEXT TWO HOURS, we talk more. He tells me all about football, and I tell him about music. It's strange, but I think because of our age difference, it feels more like we're just hanging out.

When the bill comes, he's quick to pay with a stern look. "Before you assume that I'm high-rolling it, just know that I got lucky. I grew up in the suburbs, nothing much, but I had a good family, and my world changed purely because of football."

I can only nod, as I can't relate. "Well, this has been interesting."

"I wish we could both stay, but I know you want to get back, and I should too and beat the weekend traffic to the lake."

"It's not that I'm eager to escape, well, not like I was when I first arrived. It's just I'm meeting someone." Why I bring up Lucy, I'm not sure.

Hudson seems to pick up on the fact that I'm thinking of a woman. "Oh yeah, not a girlfriend but someone special."

I rub the back of my head. "Kind of complicated."

"Listen, don't ever take dating advice from me. Like, never. But if you were to ask, then take away at least one thing—it's only complicated if you make it that way."

A sound escapes my mouth, as he has no idea. "It's more that she has three overprotective brothers."

"Ahh, nice. Not easy, but not impossible. Do I need to send a bodyguard or maybe some season tickets to lessen the blow?" Hudson speaks like we're friends, and maybe the last two hours have proven that my hesitations are a thing of history.

"You haven't met a Blisswood."

He stills for a second, and I could swear a hint of recognition washes over his face. "If she's worth pursuing then it will all be fine. Every brother wants their sister to be happy," he promises.

I shrug a shoulder. "I know, but I'm not sure I'm the one for her."

"Why? Your genetic good looks and charm are only doing you favors." Hudson crosses his arms, still invested in our conversation.

Because I'm not enough, I want to answer. "Maybe." The moment comes when I know he is going to ask, and I beat him to the punch. "I guess we'll have contact."

A smile spreads on his face. "I passed the test?"

"Something like that."

We both stand and walk in the direction of the parking lot. He squeezes my shoulder, and I imagine this is what it's like when fathers want their sons in their life. "We can text and figure out when is a good time," he suggests.

"Sure."

He presses his key to his Range Rover, and I press the key to my pickup truck. Both cars resemble two different people, yet I don't feel like we're so far off as I imagined we would be. Hudson is down to earth and different to me in some ways and alike in others.

Hudson turns to me. "I guess this is us. Do we hug this out or a handshake or simply a fist bump? I have no fucking clue the protocol, my excuse of the day."

Our hands come out to connect and then we find

ourselves in an award-winning half-hug that is both manly and awkward.

"We'll work on that," he jokes before patting my arm once more then saying bye.

When I'm back in my car, finally with a chance to breathe and think alone, I recall the last few hours, and while I feel more stable than when I arrived, I still feel a wish to have done something with my life to make him more proud of me. And I sigh when I begin to re-question if letting him into my life is a good thing or not. I don't have a good track record of parents in my life; why would that luck change?

My drive back is smooth, with the sun disappearing and replaced by low gray clouds with sprinkles hitting the windshield. By the time that I make it back to Bluetop, summer rain is in full swing.

Arriving at my house, I park in the driveway because Lucy's car is here.

A smile plays on my lips because she's here like she promised. Then dread hits me because today has been about clarity, and one thing that needs transparency is Lucy and me.

She's sitting on my porch, watching the rain, and her eyes greet me before her mouth even opens. Fuck, who knew that today the hardest part would be the conversation that I'm about to have.

15

LUCY

Drew slowly walks to me, despite the rain falling in a steady stream. All day, I've thought of him and hoped that meeting Hudson would be everything he would want it to be, but I don't think Drew even knew what to expect.

"I knew you would be here," he tells me as he steps up onto the porch.

"How did it go?" I ask. I want to kiss him hello, but I feel like I need to let him lead the way. He must have a lot of thoughts to decompress.

Drew sits down on the loveseat on the porch, and I follow him. He sighs as he sinks into the chair, and his hand finds my thigh as we both look out at the rain.

"It went easier than I thought, or at least not as bad as it could have gone. He's laidback, yet outgoing."

I look at him to study his mood, while he continues to look straight ahead. "You'll see him again?"

"Yeah, I think so."

"What did you talk about?"

He shrugs. "A lot of stuff. I don't know, though, it's only one meeting. Let's see if he shows for a second."

"Why wouldn't he?"

Drew draws his eyes to my own. "Because it would be too easy if suddenly I get to have it all. Life isn't like that for me."

I scoff at his theory and reangle my body so I can focus on him intently. "What do you mean?"

He adjusts his body so his body also faces me. "I don't know. Forget it."

"No. Say it," I request, adamant.

"What are we doing, Lucy? You and me?" His eyes feel heavy on me.

I feel like our conversation is about to take a turn. "I don't know because you're afraid. Just like you're afraid of letting Hudson in. I don't understand why."

His hand comes up to caress my cheek, and it feels soft yet sad. "You deserve more than me."

A bolt races to my heart, because fear overtakes me that this is Drew pushing me away again. "Did something happen with Hudson that makes you even more wrong?"

His hand falls from my cheek, and he moves to stand. "Nothing that isn't already the truth. I'll give you a reason to leave or you'll realize that you want more than I can give."

Quickly, I'm up on my feet, and I feel my temper flaring. "In case you haven't noticed, you've pushed me away for years and I'm still standing before you. And I don't want more, I want you."

"You're Lucy, and you've always been destined for someone who is going to give you the world, complete with white picket fence."

I step forward and my hand comes up to point a finger at

him. "Are you blind? You're not broken, you're stronger than I ever could be."

Now he looks at me, puzzled, and steps closer. "You're strong, Lucy."

I snicker and shake my head, feeling tears sting my eyes. "I'm cursed, that's what I am." Turning my back to him, I let a tear fall because I'll hate my life right now if I lose him too.

He grabs my arm and encourages me to look at him, but I shake his effort away. "You and I are the same, Drew. You think people desert you, and I uproot people's lives. My brothers pretend everything is okay, but they look at me and realize our mother is gone because of me. Grayson was dragged back to Bluetop because of me, and Knox couldn't ride off into the sunset so quick because of me. The list could go on. If you want to push me away, then fine, but come up with a better reason. Because if you think you're broken, then I am shattered just as much as you, and truthfully, I find that perfectly fitting."

As I try to walk away and head down the steps, Drew is quick to reel me back in, his hands cradling my face. "You're not a curse, nor are you damaged. Your mother was a sad fate, Grayson came back by choice only to end up with the life he wanted, and fuck Knox, he would have found any reason not to make a relationship run smoothly." He grabs both of my shoulders to ensure I look at him. "Because of you, beautiful things happen, and I don't want to let you down."

"Then don't start by pushing me away."

The corner of his mouth curves up. "The whole drive back, my head has been a mess, yet clear too. Is that possible? I don't want to mess up this chance. I don't want to wake up one day and realize that I don't get both, a father and you. I wish you didn't come back, and I wish I didn't kiss you, because now I know that I can't let you go. This is taking the biggest fucking chance because you're the last one I want to lose."

He leans down to kiss me, his arms engulfing my waist to pull me tight against his body. His kiss feels like a confirmation, with his tongue sweeping along my bottom lip and dipping into my mouth to touch my own.

I feel a fire take over him, and he hoists me up, my legs wrapping around his waist, and we walk to the door. I ignore his attempts to try and unlock the door, as I'm too busy kissing his neck.

The moment we're inside, we begin to pull and yank clothing off one another. We stumble as we travel in the direction of his bedroom, and my body feels alive and eager. I know we're about to head over a cliff, but right now, we just want to get lost in one another.

His shirt is already on the floor when I discard my tank top. I'm wearing a matching hot-pink bra and panties, something he approves of, because he's on his knees, peeling my jean shorts down my legs, and he groans when he notices the lace.

Then he pulls me up, inviting me to wrap my legs again around him. Bare skin to skin, his hard boxer-covered cock pressing against my lace, and I feel my juices coating the fabric.

"I need you on the bed," he says against my lips, trying not to break our kiss.

"I need you inside of me," I reply against his mouth.

The feeling of the cotton duvet against my back is a welcomed foundation because we were both unbalanced trying to undress and make our way to his bed.

My arms splay against the mattress above my head, stretching my body, offering everything to Drew.

His warning glare is enough to make my pelvis tip up to seek out more. I want him to touch and lick me everywhere, but most of all, I want him deep inside of me now, making me his again. The feeling of his lips dragging down my body in a hurried, yet deliberate move causes needy sounds to escape from my lips.

"I want to bury myself into your pussy. I need you to come on my tongue before you come on my cock." His hand sweeps under my body to squeeze my ass. "I'm going to do everything to you."

I gape at his suggestion, which makes him flash me a half-grin. "I swear to God, Lucy, we'll do every little thing, but right now I need to be inside of you. Deep as can be because we're doing this. You, me." His mouth slams onto my mouth as his hand roams down to my pussy.

My entire body feels a thousand jabs of electricity celebrating inside of me. In response, I feel myself relaxing into a world of pure ecstasy. "I'm yours, so go on."

Drew raises his brows at me, a form of question about birth control, I know it. "Do I need to grab…" It trails off.

"We're fine on all fronts. Right?"

"Right."

I can't touch him fast enough, and my hand is between us, sliding the fabric down so his cock can spring free. I lick my lips from the pure image. Smooth, thick, and mine.

His fingers hook onto my fabric to pull down the lace, and he tosses it to the floor. Sitting up, he helps me unclasp my bra until that too flies into the air and lands on the pile. Our mouths meet for another fervent kiss. We're both greedy in this moment, wanting to head straight for more.

Lying on my side, I look over my shoulder as he moves in behind me, and he kisses me, with his hand spreading my legs open. His fingers slide along my slit, seeking to tease me and feel that I'm ready.

"Go on," I urge.

Drew holds my head, gently wrapping a hand in my hair to ensure my mouth is available, and our eyes meet.

"Look at me," he warns me right as I feel him slide slowly inside of me. I want to close my eyes to focus on the sensation, but our unbreakable gaze is enough to make me clench around his cock.

I moan and press against him, my entire body reacting without conscious thought.

He thrusts inside of me, out, then drives back in. His fingers travel my body, pinching a nipple, circling my clit, I think I've lost my mind, and only his grunts remind me that I'm on earth.

We move together, and I remind myself that I'm his, and he will be the only man ever to touch me again.

Our lips fuse as we continue on our quest. I nearly scream into his mouth when the tip of Drew's cock hits a spot inside me that's new, but extremely sensitive in a way that only makes me want more.

"I can't get enough of this." He kisses my shoulder, as if his tender touch will balance his cock pumping inside me.

"I'm getting there," I breathe out.

It only makes him quicken all his movements on my body. "Touch yourself," he whispers the demand, and my fingers are quick to take over his pattern on my clit. His hips hold me firmly in place. "Almost... there." He moves without regret inside of me, and that alone sends me over the edge.

And not far behind me is Drew jolting inside of me as I convulse around him, letting go.

We both shudder and collapse. He kisses the back of my shoulder as my body goes slack, and he stays inside of me.

Looking behind me, our eyes meet before we share a gentle kiss on the lips. "Mmm, stay inside of me."

He chuckles deep and low. "I don't know how to leave."

"You may have to find a way; I'm not spending the night."

His face fills with disappointment, and I know the next part of our night is about to hit us.

16

LUCY

I lie carefully in bed and watch Drew enter the room, completely naked. He has a towel in his hand and comes to sit on the mattress then reaches between my legs to wipe me clean.

"It might get a little messy otherwise," he jokes.

I take the towel from his hand to finish the job and then throw it to the side, because no way am I leaving this bed anytime soon. Even though I know that staying the night isn't going to happen unless I can think of an excuse to send to Brooke, I get comfortable in bed.

Drew rests his head on the pillow and invites me to lie against his chest.

"I love summer rain," I hum.

We lie there, with early evening light and the sound of rain and thunder, the scene of my dreams.

He kisses the top of my head and strokes my hair as he stares at the ceiling. "Me too. It's relaxing. Or could be you naked in my bed, both are great options." An audible exhale leaves his mouth, and he seems to be sinking into rest. "What a day."

"A good day?"

"Very."

I kiss his chest, and I begin to study his body because I like mapping the lines of his muscles in my head.

"I'm telling your brothers."

My eyes flick up to look at him. "Really?"

He doesn't change his tone or actions. "If we're really going to do this then I'm not going to sneak around behind their backs."

I flip my body to rest my chin against his chest. "It wasn't a problem the last two weeks."

"Wasn't a great feeling, trust me. Plus, I don't know… I wasn't sure this is what would happen."

"Okay, we can tell them together."

At last, he peers down at me. "No, Lucy. Just me and them."

I growl at his intention to keep me out of the situation. On one hand, I have no problem with them knowing, but now that it's happening, it's slightly scary. "Fine."

"Grayson is going to kill me… or Knox. Enjoy me while you can," he jokes.

Playfully, I kick his calf before hooking my leg over his body and feeling his cock twitch. "They won't kill you. Just tell them after they have food in them." I listen to his heart-beat for a few ticks, and it confirms how lucky I am. "We won't have to sneak around."

"I can keep you overnight." His dimples show because he's smiling to himself.

"I would like that very much." I give him a peck on the lips.

Half of my body moves up to look for my clothes. "So far out of reach," I groan.

"Good. I like you naked more."

"I'm sure, but I need to get dressed in order to drive back. I can stretch out this evening another two hours maybe before Brooke or Grayson send the Sherlock Holmes texts."

Drew lifts his hips, and it makes his dick slide between my folds. It takes me by surprise and a sound of pleasure escapes me.

"We'll need those two hours." He grins. "I have more to do."

I squint one eye and raise the brow of the other. "Oh yeah? You know, for someone who almost came home very gloomy, you seem to be in a better mood. Should I be worried that tomorrow you'll have a classic Drew flip-out?"

"Nah. I'm taking the plunge. All in," he promises.

"As in 'yes, Lucy Blisswood, you're the one and only?'" My hands come to my heart for theatrics.

"Your pussy too. It's the one and only."

I can't help but giggle at that as I move to straddle him.

"A fucking goddess you are." His hands travel up my obliques, and he sits half up. To tease me, he quickly latches his mouth onto a nipple, then lets go. "I can't get enough of you." He falls back onto the pillow and watches me.

"Why, thank you, I can't get enough of your body either." I lean down to kiss his stomach and shimmy my body lower, allowing me ample room to tease around his cock. "I think I might be hungry." My eyes toy with him as I dart my tongue out to lick a line from below his navel then lower.

"Lucy." I love when my name dances in his voice.

I lick from the base of his cock up to the tip, then I take his tip into my mouth just like a lollipop, and I put in effort to make a pop sound when I let his tip go. Wiggling my body over his cock, I give him a teasing look.

Drew grabs hold of me by the middle and pulls me flat

against his body. "You're making it really hard not to keep you in bed all night, consequences be damned."

"Mmhmm."

"I'm torn because I love you naked in my bed, but maybe I should be more adamant you put on some damn clothes because we will both lose our minds." He grins as he interlaces our hands against the pillow.

"Shh, rest your eyes. You seem a little touchy," I taunt him.

But we fall into a new relaxing scene of lying in bed again, minus distractions.

In my head, various moments flood through my memory. "You never let me go anywhere upset."

"Huh?"

"I was once at a party, you were too. I think it was someone who was in your year at school who was back from college and threw a party. We were all there, and I was upset. You took me home and wouldn't let me leave by myself. The whole drive you said nothing at all. Why?"

Our eyes catch, and I see the faint recognition in his pupils. "I was too scared that I would ruin our silence. It was a perfect silence, and you were too young to touch. It was the safest option... I was drawn to you the moment you glanced up from your game of beer pong and looked at me like I mattered."

"And you looked at me as if I was invincible." He wraps his arms around me, giving me a hug. "Everyone was walking on eggshells around me. My dad had just died, and my friends seemed to think that I would break. But you, well, you treated me like I could be the one to break someone."

I hear him smile; I don't see it as I'm too busy burying my face against his chest. "You could. Still can."

"And I look at you the same way."

"Enough sentimental crap, Lucy. I've been through enough today. I just need to hold you, and maybe bury myself inside of you once more."

I sigh. "I don't think I can leave this bed. I'm glued to you."

"Good. Well, not quite good yet. Would you rather your brother finds out on my terms instead of storming through the door looking for you?"

"Either way, I have a feeling it'll be memorable. Are you sure I shouldn't be there?" I double-check.

He whistles in disapproval. "No, absolutely not. I think when they connect the dots in their heads that it'll be less traumatizing if they don't see us side by side. Besides, let the men have our discussion."

I chortle at that answer. "And on that note, I'm going to get dressed." He grumbles in response as I begin to rustle in his arms to slide out of bed.

Drew does take a moment, but then he slides out of bed too and finds clothes to throw on.

After we're both dressed, we walk together to the front door, his arm around me because I'm his. Turning in his arms before he opens the door, I can't hide this smile that wants to spread. "I'm happy you had a good day. Maybe life is finally taking a new direction for us. We're where we finally should be. I mean, the things we wanted, they're ours for the taking."

His thumb and long finger hook under my chin to tip my mouth up in his direction. "I hope so, because I've never had a fantasy turn into reality." He cements our lips with a kiss.

Everything about tonight is warm and makes my heart near gooey. I'll be lying awake all night in excitement.

"Night, boyfriend," I say, testing the waters with that title.

His face makes a few funny expressions as he contemplates what he just heard. "Not bad."

We kiss once more before I leave.

———

It's Monday, and it's the big day. I emerge into the kitchen to see that Brooke is folding laundry, and the girls are busy playing in the play area off the living room.

I slide onto the stool next to Brooke and casually grab a few of Rosie's shirts to fold. "Out of curiosity, was my brother in a good or bad mood this morning when he left?"

"Definitely a *good* mood." Brooke seems to be recalling something in her head.

Doing my best to scrape the image that she just insinuated from my brain, I focus on the intel that I need. "Okay, so he won't probably want to kill someone if he were to receive, I don't know, let's say news about his sister?" I continue my quest to fold laundry.

Brooke, meanwhile, stops and drops a pair of socks into the basket. "Oh no, it's happening, isn't it?"

"What do you mean?" I play dumb, but inside I'm ready for the whole world to know.

She smiles at me then nudges my arm with her own. "There's a guy."

I nod.

"We know him."

My eyes grow big, and I tip my head to the side.

It takes a second before Brooke is squealing. "Oh my God. This is really happening. You and…" She looks around the room to make sure nobody is listening. "I knew it!"

"You think Grayson will share your joy?"

Brooke continues to smile. "Nope." Her P pops, and she continues with the laundry. "Or rather, if he doesn't kill Drew then you have two other brothers up to the challenge."

My excitement falters, and I sigh as I grab my phone that I had set on the counter. Quickly I send a text to Drew.

Me: Good luck! Grayson is totally in a good mood... text me as soon as it's over. And whatever you do, if they say they want to discuss it in the barn, do NOT go there. It's a trap... and there's rope there...

I debate on adding a thumbs-up emoji for encouragement but then delete it. Turning my phone face down, I hope for a miracle.

17

DREW

Gripping the steering wheel of my car, I remind myself that there is no other way. Eventually, the Blisswood brothers will figure out who Lucy is seeing, and I should get ahead of the game and tell them now.

Blowing out a breath, I open my car door and step out onto the gravel parking lot at Olive Owl. It's clear blue skies and sun. Bennett is busy unloading the back of his pickup when he looks up at me. "Hey! Haven't seen you all weekend."

I approach him slowly, with caution. I scratch the back of my neck and try to play it cool. "I was a bit busy. Need some help there?"

He hauls a box onto the ground. "Nah, almost done. Besides, I could use a break. Want to grab a coffee with me?"

I hesitate because Bennett is the last in the order of who I need to inform. I figured tackling the lion first is the best approach, that being Grayson, because I owe him the most. "Maybe later. Grayson is around, right?"

Bennett stalls and then seems to study me before a sly smirk forms on his face. "Telling him about Lucy, huh?"

Immediately, I look at him, surprised, and he picks up on this. "Kelsey has a theory she shared."

"Okay, and…" I'm waiting for him to finish that sentence.

He leans forward to nudge my shoulder with his fist. "I'm not surprised and saw it coming."

"You're not mad?" I'm completely confused right now. I knew he would be the easiest to talk to but not a freaking walk in the park.

Bennett steps back and leans against his truck. "Nah. Besides, I know Grayson and Knox will be enough crazy that you don't need me added to the mix. That doesn't mean I'm not going to watch this shit go down." He grins.

I take in his words and nod very slowly. "Assuring," I say, sarcastic.

"Grayson is checking on Astro for Rosie. Good luck." He indicates his head to the side field where, sure enough, Grayson is feeding Astro a carrot.

I turn to walk away, but then stall to look at Bennett once more. "Just remember that I babysit your boys, in case anyone mentions murder," I remind him.

Bennett chuckles and resumes his task of unloading his car.

Walking over to Grayson, I feel a swirl of nerves in my stomach. In my fantasy world, I've rehearsed this scene a thousand times, but I never imagined that it would become reality.

Grayson looks up from feeding Astro and smiles at me. "There you are. I was wondering if you were checking on the crew at the other site or if you had an errand or something."

In truth, I did run some errands at the hardware store, and then I grabbed a coffee at Bear Brew to mentally prepare for what may be my last day on earth.

"Yeah, errands and things. Listen, can we talk for a second?"

Heading straight into it surprises even Grayson, and he looks at me with concern as he steps away from the horse whose head is peeking over the fence.

He wipes his hands together. "Sure, everything okay?"

Deep breath. "It's about Lucy."

His face floods with worry. "What about her? Is this about college? There's something she isn't telling us. Damn it, I knew it," he begins to list his thoughts, and his hand comes up to rub his forehead.

Just say it, Drew.

"Lucy and I are together."

Grayson pauses as he registers my words. His entire body language changes as he stands taller, and his eyes grow... fierce. "You and Lucy?" His voice is calm, but I can tell inside he's flipping out.

I lick my lips and breathe. "Yes."

"For how long?" His eyes don't blink, but I can see he's clenching his jaw.

"Since she came back. I wanted you to find out from me and not some other way," I explain.

Nothing. He says nothing.

That is until, "Knox!" he yells, and before I can contemplate what is happening, Grayson is storming off in the direction of the main house. I quickly follow, and on the journey, Bennett notices the scene and joins me in pursuit of Grayson who is on—fuck me—a war path.

I feel like I may actually be seeing my life flash by, with my untimely end happening in the kitchen where Knox is sitting on a chair with his wife Madison sitting on his lap.

"We need to talk," Bennett states as he heads to the coffee pot. He seems to be calm-ish.

"Can you give me a minute?" I implore and rake a hand through my hair because I feel I need to explain more.

"Fine, then let's talk about this and lay down the damn truth." Grayson has a sharp tone, almost out of character.

"What brings everyone to Olive Owl on this fine day," Knox greets us, almost more unamused that we're interrupting a moment between him and his wife. Madison seems confused as she slides off his lap and returns to her chair.

"We discovered some intel that needs to be shared and discussed," Bennett informs everyone as he takes a sip of his coffee, casual as can be.

Knox holds a hand up. "Okay, but can we chill out, because my brain right now can't process too much."

"Him and her. Them," Grayson states with a steely look.

"Them who?" Knox asks as he throws a chip that was on his lunch plate into his mouth.

I cut in. "Knox, I can explain."

Knox looks between everyone, completely lost. "Clue me the fuck in. Why would I care about them? Is this about Drew with some girl?"

Bennett chuckles almost sarcastically. "Oh man, here we go," he mutters.

Grayson shakes his head. "Because that some girl?" His eyes go wide, as if Knox should figure it out faster.

Knox looks between his brothers and then at his wife who seems to have figured it out a lot faster than Knox has, because her mouth gapes open and her hand comes to cover her lips; I swear she's smiling too.

Knox looks at me, then his brothers, then back at me. "Lucy," he manages to seethe out.

"Bingo," Bennett adds in his commentary.

Grayson and Knox both look at one another with heated

eyes, almost as if they have been preparing for this day and are trying to decide who will do the honors of killing me.

"You're sleeping with my little sister?" Knox manages to ask the question and not blink.

"It's not what you think," I attempt to defuse the situation.

Knox stands up out of his chair. I have no idea what is running through his mind, but it looks like a lot. "Then you better explain, and fast," he orders. Madison reaches out for his hand to stop him, but he ignores her.

Looking around the room, I know this is my only chance. "It was always going to be her, and now Lucy is back and we're finally figuring it out. We're together, we're going to be together. And I know you think she probably deserves better, but you get me."

"Are you fucking kidding me?" Grayson seems fumed as he crosses his arms and leans against the counter.

Bennett seems surprised by Grayson's mood. "Whoa, simmer down. You can't be that blind. How did you not know this day was coming?"

Grayson looks to Bennett with a pointed look. "We welcomed Drew into our family, he's family. Hell, I don't think I know a life where he isn't in the picture. Then this happens. He has the audacity to start dating our sister without asking my permission first. Fuck this."

"Hold up." Bennett brings his hand up to try and calm Grayson. "You're not pissed they're together. You're pissed because Drew didn't go traditional and ask for your permission to date our sister first?"

"Yes!"

Bennett starts to laugh, and relief hits me, maybe I even want to smile too.

Knox pipes up. "Are you both fucking kidding me? Bennett doesn't seem to care, Grayson is going Mr. 1950s on us, and nobody seems to acknowledge the pure fact that I have the image of Drew and Lucy, doing—ah, I can't even say it, but it's seared into my brain right now." Knox rubs his temples and seems to be taking the news the worst.

I step forward, attempting to remind everyone that I'm in the room. "It happened, and it's happening. I know it's complicated."

Knox shakes his head. "Yeah, it is. Have we all considered what happens if you two don't work out?"

I would lose it all. The girl, the family, the life I'm trying to build. "I know, but I'm taking the chance."

"You really want to go down this road?" Knox asks me as his chest moves up and down. Clearly, he's affected by this news.

The room grows silent as everyone looks at me. "Yes."

Knox looks at me with his nostrils flaring, debating what to say, but he doesn't take long. "Damn it," Knox grumbles and walks out of the room.

"Give him a minute," Bennett suggests.

I look at Grayson who sighs then grabs a plate to make himself a sandwich; he seems to have calmed.

"Uhm, sandwich anyone?" Madison smiles nervously. I forgot she was here.

I shake my head no, and instead slowly approach the kitchen island that acts as a safe barrier between Grayson and me, to focus my energy on him.

"You're okay with me and Lucy?"

He busies himself with preparing a sandwich. "You think you're not good for Lucy? That's crazy, you're exactly the kind of guy I would hope she ends up with. You have a strong work ethic, you're part of our family, and I can watch you like a hawk on a daily basis... Doesn't mean I'm not scared shitless that it'll go wrong. But you and her are not the issue.

My issue is that you felt you could start something with her without first checking with me. So, I'm waiting…" He flops a piece of cheese onto his sandwich.

Bennett chuckles. "He isn't going to be a happy camper until you ask."

Looking between everyone in the room, I can find humor in this. Grayson is going to make me grovel a little, which causes me to try and hide a smile.

"Grayson, I would… I'm asking to take Lucy… out on a date, to date her?" There is a question in my tone because I have no clue if I'm doing this right.

"A little late, but better than never. What do you plan on doing on this date?" He takes a bite of his sandwich.

I scoff a sound because he can't be serious. "Dinner." I sound almost puzzled.

Bennett's grin doesn't fade as he watches this scene unfold.

"Fine, but I expect you to get her flowers and that you take her somewhere nice."

Madison snorts a laugh. "I really wish I was filming this, but the funniest part is Grayson isn't even joking." She smiles at me as she leaves the kitchen. "Just give Knox a little time."

"Actually, I'll go outside and find him if Grayson is done with his interrogation."

"For now." He's serious, but then I see the hint of a grin.

I look at everyone and fold my lips in, relieved that it's over. Two out of three isn't half bad.

When I reach outside, I find Knox sitting on a chair on the patio. I remind myself that I knew not everyone would be welcoming to the idea of me and Lucy.

"Knox," I say as I grab the chair near him and sit down.

His gaze snaps in my direction and his arms cross his chest. "I swear to God there is some juju or some shit on this property to ensure I can never have a normal day when news hits me."

"I'm sorry. I didn't know how to tell you."

"You've been sneaking around with her?"

"Yes."

A dissatisfied sound escapes him, and he looks forward. "It'll suck if things don't work out. You're supposed to be my friend."

"What if it does work out?"

Knox's lips purse together, as if maybe he likes that idea. "We all know you and Lucy have a connection. I just thought you would leave it at that."

Leaning forward, my elbows land on my knees. "I can't. I tried, but I can't."

"Then I guess this is where we are."

We sit there in silence until Pretzel comes padding along, and he sits between us, the sound of his panting keeping us alert.

"I don't want to lose a friend," Knox says.

"Me neither," I say honestly.

I pet Pretzel's head, now believing in the power of therapy dogs, because this big boy is calming the shit out of Knox who wanted to kill me a few minutes ago.

"Our next boxing session is going to be brutal, isn't it?" I attempt to joke.

Knox glances at me with serious eyes, his look hardened. "Lucy isn't a kid anymore, but I'll be damned if I let her make a mistake."

"You think she's making a mistake with me?"

"No. But there is no way in hell she'll have the incentive to go back to college now."

Standing up, I debate what else to say, but Knox is maybe the one to understand. "She isn't making up an excuse. She's burned out, Knox. And for what it's worth, I don't want her to give up either. But it won't be because of me if she doesn't go back."

Knox slowly nods. "I know, but I've always had it in my head that Lucy wanted to go into the big world, travel, and we would have to plead for her to come back. I never thought she would be the one begging to stay. I hope you both know what you're getting yourselves into." He stands. "All I can say is that I hope for all our sakes that this works out, because right now I'm still pretty pissed and need to wrap my head around this."

I knew not everyone would be on board so easily, and Knox needing time is something I prepared for. That doesn't mean it hurts any less. Bennett and Grayson are accepting, with hesitation, but they're all right. Knox has yet to get there; it's disheartening, but not a deterrent.

At least everything is out in the open now.

No more sneaking around, and things can be easier.

Yet, when I show up to Grayson's house to pick up Lucy for our date, it's anything but.

18

LUCY

I heard the doorbell. Why did I hear the doorbell?

Drew normally just walks right into Grayson's house; he even has the security code. I mean, literally, Drew is part of this family, it's why he kept me off-limits for years. So why did he just ring the doorbell to pick me up?

Ignoring my confusion, I grab my little jean jacket in case it cools off later. Grabbing my lip balm, I coat my lips once more with the light pink shade. I'm wearing just a simple blue cotton dress and some sandals for whatever Drew has in store for our date.

An actual date... in public. Where the townspeople of Bluetop can go running to my brothers to report back. A wide smile stretches on my mouth from that thought.

Exiting my room, I hear it already before I reach the stairs.

My brother is being an ass.

"Those are good plans for the night, I approve. Though I'm not sure she's really a sunflower type of person," Grayson informs Drew.

Brooke tsks her husband. "Don't listen to him, he's just

jealous that someone here brought a woman flowers and it isn't him."

"It's okay," Drew assures her.

Rolling my eyes humorously, I walk down the stairs, and suddenly I feel several pairs of eyes landing on me.

"Sunflowers are perfect." I reach the bottom of the stairs, and all of my attention lands on Drew. He's wearing a dark blue button-down shirt. It's different, he's more a t-shirt kind of guy, but the effort is going to be well rewarded later, because he looks hot.

Drew offers me the flowers and suddenly I feel like I'm in high school again, when everyone would watch every time a guy picked me up, even if we were just friends. "You look good." His eyes have a glint to them as he compliments me.

I take the flowers, pluck one out, and slide it into my hair behind my ear.

"I expect her to be back by midnight," Grayson informs Drew.

We all laugh until we realize Grayson isn't joking.

"Don't wait up, I won't be home tonight," I confidentially tell my brother.

His jaw tightens slightly, and he swallows. "As in you're staying at…"

"Drew's." I raise my brows at him.

Drew clears his throat slightly as he awkwardly scratches the back of his neck. "Lucy," he nervously hisses with a smile.

Brooke rubs her husband's back. "Which is completely fine, as they are two consenting *adults*, and I believe the rule was no sleepovers *here*."

"This is the first date…" Grayson puffs out a breath.

I proudly walk to Drew and grab his arm. "Hardly. You know the timeline, Grayson. See ya in the morning."

Quickly, I yank Drew's arm and get us out of the house. I beeline it to the front seat of Drew's truck, but Drew stops me before I can open the door by putting his hand on the handle.

"I can do that," I insist.

Drew steps closer to me, and for the first time tonight, I can feel him. He has this smoldering look that is new, to me at least. "Not a fucking chance. I'm positive your brother is peeking out of the living room window to check if I pass the test on date manners. Especially after that little stunt you pulled inside. Should we just hire an airplane to fly a sign in the sky that says we're sleeping together?" His hands grip my obliques, and I love how he touches me without hesitation.

I grin and play innocent. "Setting expectations, that's all."

"Oh yeah?" He steps closer and tips his head down to kiss me quick yet smooth. "Get in the car, Lucy." He opens the door and holds it open for me.

Soon we're driving off, but I actually have no clue to where. "Big plans?"

"Bowling then dinner. Nothing too fancy."

"I love it, actually."

He interlaces our hands on the middle console of the car. "Is it bad if I don't take Grayson too seriously?"

I chuckle. "I don't."

Drew grows quiet for a second. "Knox is pissed."

I squeeze his hand. "He isn't angry. He just needs to… I'm not sure what he needs. It shouldn't stop us."

"Still sucks."

"It'll be fine eventually. And tonight, I don't particularly want to talk about my brothers." My finger circles over the back of his hand. His hands are strong and calloused from all the work he does.

He side-glances at me with an approving look. "Deal."

———

THE THING with guys taking women bowling is that it is the easiest excuse to embrace all night.

"Let me help you," Drew tells me for my tenth try. His arms wrap around me as he helps me carry the weight of the ball back.

"I'm not sure I can do it."

He lifts our arms back before sweeping them forward to let go of the ball. It causes the ball to roll down the lane in a perfect line—because he has good aim.

"See? I need your help," I pout.

Drew lets me go and walks to the shelves with the balls. "No, you don't." He picks up a red ball that weighs more than the one I use. "I know you're playing me." A sheepish grin stretches on his mouth.

I pretend to be shocked. "What would make you think that?"

"Because I know you've bowled before with your brothers. Remember Thanksgiving weekend your freshman year of college?" He raises a brow at me.

Shoot. My face drops as I fall onto the chair. "I forgot about that. Blisswood competitiveness at its finest." My brothers decided family bowling was something worth a try, and it lasted for four hours.

Drew leans down to peck my lips with a kiss. "But I love that you always want my arms around you." He swings his ball and turns before he even gets a chance to see that he made a strike.

"They're warm arms."

He joins me on the chair next to me. "Not your idea of a real date?"

"No, I love this. Kind of relaxing, you know? Get out

some aggression and reduce stress." I lean my head against his shoulder.

"Getting hungry for dinner? I made reservations at this little place by the river." He kisses the top of my head.

I smile and hum as I hold his arm closer. "Sounds romantic, but you know nachos and chili dogs here at the bowling alley would suffice."

He snorts a laugh. "Really? You don't want me to go all out on this dating thing?"

"Oh, I do, but tonight I think I just want to keep you to myself and eat something quick so we can go back to your place. Do you think we can do a rain check on the romantic-dinner part?" I request. Maybe it's selfish, but I just want to be in a bubble with him and away from the world.

Drew throws me a skeptical glance, but then a grin stretches on his mouth. "Normal hotdog? Or the works?"

"Works, please." I give him an overdone smile.

Fifteen minutes later, I'm chomping on my food as we sit side by side and watch people bowl. I can tell that Drew is looking at me oddly. "Hey, I'm not a princess. I can appreciate a good hotdog," I mumble with a full mouth.

"I can tell."

"What, did you think I need a horse-drawn carriage?"

He flashes his eyes. "Nah, that would entail involving Cosmo 2.0, and we know how you get about him."

I pinch his arm. "Really, though, I don't belong on some pedestal."

His look, I can only describe it as adoration. "You have no idea how special you are." It comes out simply, but it's tinted with deep thought.

Suddenly I feel self-conscious from his remark, and I occupy myself by patting my mouth with a napkin. "Simple works, we don't always need to plan."

"You used to be a planner."

"True, but it's the little moments, the spontaneous ones, that sometimes are the best. I remember when I was eighteen, about to go off to college, and despite you rejecting me, we were still okay around each other. It was a barbecue at Olive Owl, and you were standing under the tree with the swing. We tried to make small talk, but what stood out was when you captured a lightning bug in your hands and told me if I blink, my wish will light up."

"Clever of me," he retorts.

"It was already romantic, you didn't even need to try. See, no effort needed." We both look at one with acknowledgment and soft looks until I abruptly stand and hold out my hand. "Come on, Casanova, it's time to get out of here."

He takes my hand. "Lightning bugs and you on my living room floor, preferably naked."

I kiss his cheek in approval.

———

DREW WASN'T JOKING about taking me on the living room floor. The moment we entered his house, he had me wrapped in his arms, and he guided us to the floor until I was sitting in his lap, riding him as his lips never left my own.

That was an hour ago. Now I'm lying on my side with a blanket tangled around my body, watching him as he strums his guitar. The lighting in the house is dim, and light streams in through the front window from the porch and it outlines his figure. I admire the sound of a few chords and a line or two of a song.

A half-smile stays permanently on my mouth. When he takes a break, I ask the obvious. "Are you thinking about writing another song about me?" There is a sentimental undertone in my voice.

His eyes shoot in my direction. "You know that answer."

I begin to bring my body up to sitting and slowly stand, sliding the blanket with me to cover my naked body. Taking a seat next to him, I study his fingers playing with the strings. "I love everything about it, when you play, I mean." I slide my fingers gently along his wrist. "How you hit the strings, and when you sing." We both watch my fingers drag along his skin in a circle. "That you sing about me, it's what every woman dreams about."

"Are you already trying to lead us down the rabbit hole of another round?"

"Nah, just wanted to clarify that you have talent, in case you were wondering. And for a man who doesn't always say much, you have a way with words when you play."

He shrugs off the compliment. "It just kind of comes to me."

"I get it, I have it with my writing."

Drew tries to control his laugh that wants to break free, but he manages to keep his mouth closed and cheeks tight. "I can only imagine that I play a role in your imagination."

I wiggle my brows at him.

His phone vibrating on the coffee table breaks our focus. Peering over, I'm nosy and see that Hudson's name comes up on the screen, but I don't read further. Drew doesn't seem to react and goes back to focusing on his guitar.

As much as I shouldn't push, I can't control it. "Are you ignoring him? I thought the meeting went well?"

Drew slides the instrument off his lap to place against the edge of the sofa. "It did, he's just… eager."

"Eager?" I'm puzzled.

"Keeps sending suggestions about what we can do for our

next visit. Asks a lot of questions," he recalls as he reads the message on his phone.

My lips quirk out then in. "Questions can be good. What's he asking, let me see…" I snuggle in closer to Drew to look over his shoulder. "Uhm, *how are you today* is what we humans call being polite. Why does that have you uneasy?"

He tosses the phone to the side on the couch. "I'm not uneasy, just… it's taking getting used to. With your brothers it's normal, but with Hudson… he's blood-related, you know?"

My finger taps his shoulder as I deconstruct his thought. "You haven't really had someone who is biologically related to you in your life, I get it. But it's only biology, sometimes that doesn't mean much. It's more about the bond you have. As long as you know that he's really trying to be a normal guy, I don't think he has a hidden agenda."

"I don't think so either. It's just taking some getting used to."

"Why don't you keep it easy? Bowling was relaxing, maybe try that with him?"

Drew chuckles as he leans back into the couch. "Quite a contrast to his suggestion of watching a football game together with box seats. Or going to his lake house."

"But it's you. You're a laidback guy. Let him get to know that side."

He blows out a breath. "Right."

I'm not convinced, and I shake his arm that I entwine with my own. "I bet if you take a chance then you may just let another person in your life that will be there for you."

I can feel him tense slightly; I know he isn't used to that thought. "I love your confidence." He sounds deflated. "I will see him again, I'm just…"

He's afraid.

I bring my hands to rest on his cheeks so he can't look away. "Not everything in life is out to knock you down. You also get lucky on a few things. It just so happens that you gained a very hot girlfriend and a dad all at the same time. It's possible to have both."

He begins to comb his fingers through my long hair, a feathery touch that is tender and warm.

"Your faith in this matter is strong, and I'm slightly in awe."

My lips twitch because this is personal for me. I would grab the opportunity to have had more time with many people in my life. "Because in a second you can lose it all, and then you never even got to enjoy the moments."

He understands, and he gives me a look of fondness. "Come with me?"

"To where? Paradise or into the woods?" I joke to lighten his mood.

"Next time I see Hudson, come with me." It's more a statement than a request.

Slowly I nod yes because I'll do anything for this man. And maybe as soon as Drew believes he is worthy of family, then I won't need to worry he'll eventually push me away.

19

DREW

I lean against my truck while I wait for Lucy at Olive Owl. She asked that I pick her up here, because she wanted to chat with Madison and check on Astro for Rosie. I'm positive that Lucy's become attached to that horse, even if she won't admit it.

Knox emerges from the barn with two bottles of wine in hand. He still hasn't really spoken to me since he found out the news. "Let me guess. Waiting for Lucy, my little *sister*." I hear the slight disdain in his voice as he continues to walk on, not paying much attention to me.

"Knox, is it really going to be like this now?" I ask with a barely-there humor in my voice. Partly because I want to believe that eventually he will snap out of the phase of shock.

"Today? Yes," he calls out.

As he disappears, I blow out a long breath. My irritation for the situation is short-lived when I see Lucy smiling and walking toward me. She's wearing a summer dress that is long and light yellow. For some reason, I feel like she's putting in a little extra effort today.

She walks right into my arms to kiss me, and while my

arms willingly snake around her, my eagerness to kiss her long and hard is distracted by the idea that Knox can see us.

"Ignore him," she sternly warns before leaning in to kiss me anyway.

And damn, her kiss is calming.

"Ready?" I ask when I pull away.

"Absolutely," she promises.

Perhaps deep within me, I was scared that when we stopped sneaking around an element of excitement would disappear. But it hasn't. The days go by, and I feel Lucy getting more integrated into my life. It's slightly unnerving, but also nothing short of contentment.

Now she is coming with me to see Hudson, and we're going to drive to his lake house, where he promised a low-key BBQ. I think I agreed to that setting because I'm curious about his life, but also, knowing Lucy would be with me to make the drive enjoyable made it easier to approve.

It doesn't take long for us to be on our way on this sunny Saturday afternoon.

"Everything okay at Olive Owl with Madison?" I ask.

"Peachy." Lucy looks out the window to admire the flat fields as we drive by. "We just talked about life. She casually mentioned that I could look at transferring my college credit to somewhere closer, and we talked about my plan B. Basically, she gave me a teacher talk but with complete sister-in-law vibes."

It sparks my interest. "Would you want to do that? Go to college somewhere closer?"

Her head whips in my direction. "No," she flat-out tells me. "I'm not finishing."

Even after all these weeks, I'm struggling to understand her logic. It isn't like her at all.

"You know I'm not going anywhere. If you wanted to go

back…" I would wait for her. I should have done that already all these years. Guilt hits me in the gut, because maybe if I had just been honest about my feelings from the get-go then she wouldn't be in her current situation.

"Let's not talk about it now. Today is about you and Hudson."

That reminder causes me to do a full-body scan. Luckily, the first-meeting nerves have already been ripped off like a band-aid. Nonetheless, there are a few flurries still floating inside of me.

It's a smooth ride to Lake Spark, the town where Hudson has his weekend home. Hudson texted to meet him out back, as he may not hear the doorbell and needs to keep an eye on the grill.

Arriving at his house, it's big, no doubt about that. The modern two-story build feels like he must have had someone design the property. I can tell the materials of the build are new. Distracting myself with the minor details of the infrastructure, I feel Lucy pulling my hand.

"You okay?" she checks and brings my hand to her lips for a kiss.

"Completely."

The smell of coals burning wakes me up slightly because I'm still not entirely sure that this is my life. Circling around the corner and we're met with a view of the lake and a very large patio. I can see a hot tub in the corner of my eye, and then I notice the state-of-the-art grill with Hudson smiling behind it.

"Hi!" He closes the lid of the grill. "You found it. Welcome." Hudson wipes his hands on his apron with an utterly ridiculous phrase printed on it, *This Guy Rubs His Own Meat*, but I guess it does the trick because Lucy chortles under her breath.

She leans in to whisper, "Oh my God, if this is what you look like in seventeen years then marry me now."

I flash her a concerned glare.

Lucy and I meet him halfway, and instantly he shakes Lucy's hand. "You must be Lucy."

"Yep. And you are totally his dad, I can see the resemblance." Lucy already seems to be looking between us and examining the situation. "Maybe more like brothers because, well, I'm not sure I would guess the whole father-son age dynamic."

Hudson proudly grins. "I like you already."

"Hi." I shake his hand, and I can see he wants to maybe pull me in for a hug, but I'm not really a hugger in general.

Hudson steps back, clearly reading my signals. "Drink, anyone? I have soft drinks, some specialty beers, wine?"

"Oh, no wine for me. I'm kind of tainted by the Olive Owl brand. I can't drink any other out of loyalty," Lucy muses.

"Beer is fine for me," I say and rub my chin.

I can do this, I remind myself.

Hudson grabs some drinks from an outside fridge that is near the grill. "Make yourselves at home. I'll throw the meat on the grill when we get hungry."

Offering us our drinks, we all take a seat on the lounge set. "It's... quite a view here," I remark. It's gorgeous, actually. A line of pine trees are on one side, and the water is a deep blue, not brown like many lakes around here. His dock that stretches out into the lake looks stable and a perfect spot to jump into the water.

"I know. I kind of discovered Lake Spark due to some guys in the industry. My neighbor's a baseball player, and another neighbor is a hockey player. All good guys, and we hang out when we can." Hudson drinks from his beer bottle and seems completely ready for today.

"The town looked quaint, too, when we drove through," Lucy mentions.

"Small-town feel, with tourists who flock here in the summer. In the winter, you can do a little skiing or sledding nearby. Nothing like Colorado, but decent enough. The water is a bit chilly even in the summer. So, tell me about you two, quite new?" His eyes grow in excitement.

Lucy and I look at one another, and she smiles nervously. "Yeah, something like that," I say. "Lucy is back from college."

"Just finished college, actually," she corrects me.

"Oh yeah? What's the next step?" Hudson seems genuinely interested.

I interject, "Lucy's taking a little break to figure it out."

"That makes sense." I do appreciate that he doesn't seem judgmental.

"Anyway, Lucy's brothers are the ones I told you about."

"Blisswood, right? Figured that out quite quickly with the wine reference. What else is new since we last saw one another? You don't give me much via text," he subtly teases me.

Lucy nudges my arm. "Drew isn't really a texter, and sometimes sentences in general are in short supply. *But* he is great with words in songs." She seems to be gushing over me.

"Did you bring your guitar?" he asks, maybe too excited.

I shake my head. "Nah, not today. Anyway, this place seems like a perfect escape." I still can't get my admiration for the view out of my head or maybe I'm using it as a distraction.

"It is. I'm quite lucky that I can stay out of the press

except when we have a game, but still, it's nice to get away from people."

Lucy snorts a laugh. "Drew can really relate to that. The away-from-people part, must be genetic."

I have to smile at her reference or maybe it's because I do have something in common with Hudson. "It's a good trait to have. But I guess when you coach football that you deal with a lot of assholes. Or at least I can imagine, I've only seen professional football on TV."

Hudson stands up to quickly check on the coals. "I would like to think I level with my guys, but I do need to be an ass sometimes because not all players understand the meaning of team. It was worse when I actually played football. Now as a coach I kind of have the hierarchy on my side. You should come to a game, really."

"You've mentioned. I guess maybe one time it could be fun," I admit.

"I wasn't going to show you my wall of photos and trophies to sway your decision, but I can if that helps."

"Nah, it's fine. I'll take your word that I should give the game a chance. Knox watches football, such a shame he's giving me the silent treatment now," I mostly speak to myself, but Hudson heard.

Lucy quickly explains, "Out of three brothers, one wasn't entirely on board about us. But one out of three is what I would call a win, right?"

"Completely." Hudson seems to be staring at me.

"What's on the menu?" I try to change the subject.

Hudson picks up on that. "I have chicken, figured that's safe. Plus, I kind of picked up last time that you appreciate ranch, so got a few different flavors of that too."

"Sounds good."

A little while later, we're sitting around the table and

eating delicious chicken and sides. Nothing fancy, more homestyle and hearty than anything.

Lucy clears her throat when she notices a break in our conversation about Chicago. "You should visit Bluetop, check out our quirky town. I'm sure I can get you a discount at Olive Owl," she offers and flashes her eyes at me.

"I bet. A wine tasting sounds good, and I may even need to have a charity event to arrange that could use a location. Isn't pumpkin season quite big for you guys?" While all of this information is public knowledge, it feels as though Hudson is more attuned than most people. I can't put my finger on it, but something strikes me as peculiar.

"It is. Drew helps out at Olive Owl. We need his strength to help move those little orange beasts. He's been doing it for a few years now." Lucy touches my thigh, and her words mixed with a smile feel like constant praise. I hate that kind of shit, except when she does it, because it's sincere coming from her. "Definitely visit." She insists.

My dad walking into my life. Where I live, work, and breathe on a daily basis. Nothing would be a mystery to him anymore.

"Yeah, uhm, *maybe* soon." They both seem to pick up that I'm not entirely on board.

Lucy looks between us all, then gently tosses her napkin to the side of her plate. "Excuse me, little ladies' room calls."

"Sure, inside past the kitchen to the right." Hudson nods.

Lucy smiles at him then gently hawks her eyes at me. It's her warning that I should let down a wall.

With Lucy out of sight, I look at Hudson, with the sound of birds the only noise.

"She's a good woman, you're lucky," he begins.

"Why, because in a normal world, I'm the guy she

shouldn't even look at?" I counter and hear my insecurities coming through.

Hudson grins to himself and takes another sip of his drink. "That Arrows temperament is coming out again. I just meant *any* guy who has a woman like that is lucky. Drew, I'm on your team."

Sighing, I know this. Holding my hands out, I apologize. "Sorry, still new. This. All of this."

"Got that. I'll approach you with caution and bribes of food until you fully come around. Then again, I won't apologize for trying. I see a benefit to having you in my life and vice versa. And when you let people in, you sometimes end up with the life you always wanted."

"That isn't a life I wanted." I motion to his house.

"That's a perk. No, what I mean is that life is already complicated enough; don't make the people who want to be in your life one of those complications."

God, I hear him, I do. And his sentence seems to sink into my head like a dead weight. Why can't I just let everyone in?

"How about dessert?" he offers.

He stands and grabs a plate, but quickly I stop him, with my tongue running my thoughts. "Going all-in with Lucy, I know the risk. Hell, I'm missing a boxing partner until further notice. But I'm still not sure what all-in with you looks like— other than football tickets and you hounding me for daily updates on my life or wearing ridiculous aprons while you barbecue."

A smirk forms on his mouth. "I could tell you that I'll ask how you are, or that I can't wait for birthdays or one day when you'll have a bachelor party. But those are all words. The best way to figure it out is to take a chance, and you'll figure it out on your own what I am to you."

"Doesn't exactly help with my clarity."

The line of his mouth stretches wider. "Why do you need someone else to tell you? You're an independent guy, you'll find your answer." He holds a dish up in a sort of salute before he walks away to get dessert.

He leaves me there to ponder because he's right. I've always been capable of doing things on my own. It's only when it involves adding people to my life that I become a little lost. But maybe I'm not lost at all and just need to approach my current state of life in a different way.

———

AFTER DESSERT AND MORE TALK, Lucy and I decided to head back.

Arriving at my place, we walk into the kitchen, and I slide my keys onto the counter. "It wasn't so bad, was it?"

"Not at all," she assures me honestly as she leans over the counter on her propped elbows. "You two seem like you could really have a good relationship. He is totally invested in you."

"So, not out of my orbit?" I wonder as I look at her.

"He seems like an awesome guy, and I see a few similarities. You should totally keep giving him a chance," she gushes praise.

I tap my fingers on the fridge handle. "It's good to hear you say that. Maybe I needed an outside eye to give me some perspective."

Lucy strides in my direction then softly touches my shoulder. "Throw him a bone, don't make him ask again. Send him a message thanking him for today and invite him out to Bluetop."

It takes a few beats, but I nod as I debate the thought, except there isn't anything in my head telling me not to.

Pulling my phone from my pocket, I quickly type with my thumbs on the screen.

Thanks for today. Perhaps when you have time in your schedule, you can come out to Bluetop?

"You'll probably need to tell my brothers soon. I mean, if Hudson just shows up then how will you explain it?"

I slide my phone onto the counter. "I guess telling your brothers just makes it real. They're the closest thing I have to family, and I don't want to replace that."

"You're not replacing them, nor will they see it that way. Don't let it stress you out."

She brings my hand to cover her breast over the fabric, which causes my eyes to bug out in interest. Then she uses my hand to squeeze her. "Not stressed now," I say, my voice thick with lust.

"Good." She steps closer to me, walking us to the wall. "Now, I think we need to celebrate a good day." Lucy doesn't wait for my answer, which is a groan, because she's already dropping to her knees before I have a chance to configure words.

"Want to take this to the bedroom?"

She glances up as she unzips my jeans. "No." Her tone is clipped. Her mouth trails hot breath around my boxer briefs. "I want you right here." So fucking sultry this girl.

Jesus, she darts her tongue out to lick my cock that's painfully hard.

My fingers tangle into her hair to guide her mouth. "Go on," I encourage her with a heavy breath.

She obeys and peels my shorts down just enough before her hand wraps around my length. Her grip tightens, and she gives me two strokes before she licks the head of my cock like a lollipop.

Closing my eyes, I feel her watery mouth take in my cock. Her mumbled moan is a sound of ecstasy.

"Deeper, I know you can," I request.

A surge of heat swells below my navel as I feel her swallow and suck. I may be losing my mind.

What a perfect way to end the day because it was a good day.

Mostly because Lucy was with me, which makes me want to try even harder to repair my friendship with her brother, and also because I am slowly welcoming Hudson into my life. Because maybe I can have it all, finally…

20

LUCY

Rejection.

That's exactly what I'm staring at. Finally, I heard back from the literary agent and while I knew it was a slither of a chance to get my book accepted, I was still hopeful. It still stings, even though I had realistic expectations.

I toss my phone back into my purse as I sit at the bar of Rooster Sin. This place without fail provides an atmosphere that can be the setting for a magical evening or a night you would rather forget. Something about a rundown local establishment with good music, cheap beer, and dry roasted nuts that just always provides the props to the unexpected.

Madison raises her brows at me as she plays with the straw in her cola. "You okay?"

I shrug a shoulder. "Sure." In the corner of my eye, I see where my brothers are sitting together at their own table for an afternoon drink.

My sister-in-law reaches across the table to squeeze my hand. "I don't want to press but the deadline for transferring college is the end of the week, you maybe want to look into it."

I sigh and then lean back against the stool. "Great." My tone lacks enthusiasm.

"Okay, I get the hint. New topic. How's it going with Drew?"

It's natural, the gentle smile that forms on my mouth. "Can't complain," I say, playing coy.

My eyes divert when I notice that Drew is entering the bar. Before Drew even has a chance to smile, I'm relieved, and the last few minutes seem forgotten. He tucks his sunglasses into his shirt, scans the room, then looks between Madison and me with a faint smile.

Walking to us, he greets us when he places his hand on the back of my stool. "What brings you two here?"

Truthfully, even though I knew Drew would be meeting up with my brothers, I didn't plan to come until Madison invited me. This is a chance encounter, as we don't give one another a play-by-play of what we're doing every moment. Then again, Bluetop is small, so chance encounters are a norm.

"Living the life of two jobless souls," I mundanely answer.

Madison softly laughs. "I'm on summer vacation, slightly different. But the guys are over there, and we didn't want to hear them talk sports."

"Is Knox in a good mood today?" Drew scratches his neck as he anxiously awaits an answer.

"Better than the other week. So yeah, I think you'll walk away with two legs and two arms, still attached to your body. Also, love that you're all calling a gathering at Rooster Sin, with beers and perhaps only one sentence about Olive Owl."

Her fingers hook in air quotes. "A work meeting." She smirks at him.

"It's tradition. And I'm happy to hear that I'll be left intact." He turns his attention to me. "I'm going to leave you two at it… I'm telling them about Hudson." His voice softens on that last part.

All I can do is give him a reassuring smile. "Good. I'm sure they'll order a round of the hard stuff. Maybe I will too."

He leans down to press his lips against my own. A quick kiss that still leaves me wanting to pinch myself to make sure this isn't a dream. At least something in my life is going right. I have a guy who I cook grilled cheese sandwiches for, whose shirts have become a staple of my wardrobe, and whose shampoo lingers in my hair. Not just any guy, it's Drew.

The slurping from a straw breaks my daze, causing me to blink a few times as I refocus on Madison.

"Funny how patience pays off."

I think I grow almost bashful because Madison has watched it all. From teenage crush to getting the guy. "I just hope it's forever."

"Why wouldn't it be?"

"Because it's me," I mention. Before she can ask why, her hand comes to her stomach, and she breathes with purpose. Almost as if she's trying to calm herself. "You okay?"

"Yeah… it's fine." She shakes it off then straightens her body. "I'm not sure why you feel like you need hope, because sometimes fate just steps in. And what was it he meant by telling the guys about Hudson?" Her interest is piqued.

It dawns on me that Drew's words to me may have been cryptic, considering she doesn't have all the facts, but since he's telling my brothers today then I decide to give her the vague details. "Well, you know how Drew doesn't really have parents?" She nods sadly. I continue, "That's not entirely true now. He discovered his real dad, and they've met."

Madison's mouth parts open slightly, and she glances at the guys sitting on the other side of the room before returning her stare at me. "Wow, that's big news."

I tuck a strand of hair behind my ear. "I know, but he's a really nice guy. Completely wants to make an effort with Drew."

"Hudson, you mean?"

"Yep. Actually, he's kind of a big name if you're into football," I casually state.

Her face turns confused. "Wait, as in Hudson Arrows?"

My eyes go big as I awkwardly bob my head and quirk my lips out.

"Huh." She sinks into her chair and seems to be thinking.

I brush past her moment of consideration. "It's kind of a big deal to Drew since, you know, my brothers are like his brothers. He has this whole theory in his head that makes no sense. Anyway, Hudson will come visit Bluetop soon, even Olive Owl, so we'll need to plan a whole meal and wine tasting."

"But we don't need to plan anything."

"What do you mean?"

"Hudson has already had a tour. He was at Olive Owl a few weeks ago and spoke with Knox."

Now I'm confused. "As in my brother?"

She nods and takes a sip of her drink. "Yep. Hudson wasn't there for long, maybe an hour tops. I didn't think much of it, we always have Chicago big shots stopping by."

Now a theory is forming in my own brain. Because something doesn't add up, and I feel like suddenly Knox already knows about Hudson, which makes me even more upset that he's pissed at Drew right now. Surely, he should recognize that Drew needs a friend more than ever.

But when I look up from my drink and see that Madison is tightly keeping her lips together because she's trying not to gag, then I know my thought will have to wait.

"Are you sure you're feeling alright?" I check with her and touch her arm.

She holds a finger up. "Yep. Excuse me for one sec, I'll be right back." Soon she is sliding off her chair and rushing to the bathroom in a hurry.

I debate following her, but she seems to have it under control. Instead, a growl forms in my throat when I hear my phone vibrate, and against my better judgment and my mood, I read the text.

Brooke: Hey, Rosie wants to have a birthday party for Astro. Could you help me arrange a cake?

You have got to be kidding me? Rejection, family secrets, and a fucking invite for a birthday party for Cosmo 2.0 all in one day. Breathing, I remind myself that I came back to Bluetop knowing this is the kind of craziness that I may have missed.

Except, I'm not sure Drew will see it that way.

I ignore my phone yet again today and choose not to answer. I look at my brothers and Drew sitting at a table in the corner and decide to head their way.

As I approach the group, I hear the Drew say, "There's something I need to tell you all."

Bennett sees me arrive, then looks at Drew. "Shit, you didn't learn from me and forgot birth control." Bennett seems horrified and swipes a hand through his hair, clearly panicked.

"Seriously? That's where your mind goes? No, not what

he was trying to say." I shake my head, not amused, and Bennett is instantly relieved.

I scoop Drew's hand into my own and the line of my mouth stretches slightly to give him assurance. He nods to me and then continues. "Turns out I have a biological dad out there who isn't Keith."

My brothers instantly go silent, frozen almost. A table of quiet Blisswoods is never a great thing, it's unnerving, even for the random guy sitting at the edge of the bar who turns to look. The talent to change the atmosphere is a genetic quality, I guess.

Grayson is the first to speak. "Wow, this maybe makes sense. I mean, why you and Keith were never so close."

"My real dad didn't even know, but now we've met, and he seems decent. He's going to visit Bluetop, and I would like him to meet you all." Drew's eyes are glued to his beer bottle.

A hum escapes from Grayson's mouth, then the corners of his mouth hitch up. "This is promising news, Drew. How long have you known?"

Quickly, Drew glances to me then back to Grayson. "A little while. I needed to wrap my head around it."

"It's heavy news, but you seem okay," Bennett notes.

Drew laughs humorlessly. "Now I am. Not so much when I found out."

"What's he like?" Grayson gets comfortable in his chair and already I know he will have a lot of questions.

"A few similarities to Drew, more outgoing for sure," I tell him.

Drew lets my hand go to bring his hands behind his head to huff out a distressing breath. "He was sixteen when I was born, so the age difference is kind of odd, especially when you're Hudson Arrows." His brows raise up then down.

"As in the football coach? One of the youngest coaches

out there?" Bennett double-checks. Drew slowly nods. "No shit."

My eyes land on Knox who seems awfully quiet. "Aren't you going to say something?"

Knox's eyes strike my own, but he doesn't get a chance to speak.

"It's fine. He doesn't need to say anything." Drew sounds slightly defeated.

A long silence hits our table until I decide to break it. "Family dinner at Olive Owl? Invite for Hudson?"

"Of course, we've got to show him a good time," Grayson promises.

"He's already been to Olive Owl," Knox states, with his eyes set on staring at the table, not blinking.

Drew glances to him. "No, I don't think he has."

Knox's cheeks tighten, and I can tell he's tense. Closing his eyes for a second, he gathers his thoughts. "Yes, he has. Because I've spoken to him."

Drew laughs it off. "Can't be, he said he's never been."

"Well, he's been," Knox remains adamant. "I know because I talked to him... about you."

Everyone's attention lands on Knox.

Drew's neutral face fades as he digests the news.

Knox's nostrils flare slightly as he breathes deep. "He may not want you to know he stopped by, but he did. He was looking for Grayson and got stuck with me. He wanted to thank us or check on us, I'm not quite sure. It was with good intentions."

"So why didn't you tell Drew?" I press my brother.

Inside me anger boils, but that's nothing compared to Drew who is now radiating disappointment.

"Probably because Knox is so pissed at me that he felt he didn't need to tell me—"

Knox cuts in, "That's not it at all."

"Well, I guess we know where I stand with you." Drew pushes back from the table and looks at everyone,

"There must be an explanation," Grayson tries to bring the peace.

"It's not a big deal," Knox says, throwing fuel on the fire as he looks between us all. My brother just stated the opposite of what the situation actually is.

Bennett groans at his answer.

"I need some air." Drew lowers his head in disapproval then walks in the direction of the exit.

I shake my head at my brother, but I'll deal with him later. Instead, I follow Drew.

When I make it outside into the late summer afternoon, I find Drew leaning against the brick of the building with one knee bent up and his hands in his pocket.

My hands fall to my sides. "I don't know what to say."

Drew's head lazily lolls to the side to look at me with a piercing gaze.

Stepping slowly forward, I'm cautious that I'm standing in front of a giant hazard. "If Knox says it was with good intentions, then it must've been."

"Lucy, Hudson has already lied to me, and Knox isn't exactly winning points right now either." The hurt in his voice is apparent.

"I know it must feel like a lie, but if it is really what Knox says, then that's just what parents sometimes do. Hudson is watching out for you… because he cares."

Drew crosses his arms over his chest. "Right," he scoffs.

Surveying the parking lot, I see we're alone. "Drew, don't do this. You're just trying to find a reason to push him away."

"Lucy…"

Now, I sigh, slightly irritated. "If you're going to go in a circle about not getting close to Hudson, then I'm not sure what I can say. You have people who want you in their life, and if you're never going to fully let everyone in, then what chance do I have with you?"

It grabs his attention, and his bent knee drops so he can stand tall. "I warned you that I'm no good for you."

I look up the sky as if a sign from heaven may drop into my arms. "You know what? I can't do this right now. I'm trying to be strong and supportive, but today is already dragging me under, and now my boyfriend and brother are even more at odds, all because he doesn't see that everyone is trying to do the right thing. Maybe it's an unusual way of doing it, but deep down, the intentions are pure."

Our eyes whip in the direction of the door and Knox hesitantly walks to our bubble.

"You!" I point my finger at my brother as my emotions seem to be building inside of me. "Remember when you started seeing Madison? You promised me that one day when I'm in love that you would go easy on him. You owed me that. What the fuck happened to that memo? Because you are really being an asshole right now when both Drew and I could use a pass on the friction you're throwing at us."

"Lucy, I'm sorry. Can we talk about this?" Knox attempts to defuse me.

Shaking my head furiously, I feel a hurricane brewing inside of me. A mixture of anger, sadness, and fear. I've never felt this before. As if my entire body is shattering into a puddle on the ground, and it's been in the making for months now. I'm tired and feel like tears will spring out of my eyes any moment if I don't escape. I can't even control it.

"No, talk about it with Drew. Because right now, having you two pissed off at each other is not what I need. *At all.*"

Shit. The first tear falls. Is this a nervous breakdown that I hear people talk about? Exhaustion? Burnout? Or a broken heart? So many options.

Both Drew and Knox reach out to touch my arm. "Come on, Lucy, let's get out of here." Drew seems to be concerned.

"No!" I snipe.

My brother and Drew step back.

"Is everything okay?" Madison asks as she arrives to the scene.

I feel like I'm about to start shaking. "Can you take me home?" I request and walk into her arms as my face melts into a cry.

Drew reaches out. "Lucy—"

Glancing over my shoulder as Madison leads the way, I warn the men in my life. "I don't want to see either one of you until one of you starts to be the brother that I need and the other realizes that he has an entire army of people who love him, so he needs to fucking stop finding an excuse to push everyone away."

By the time I make it to the front seat of Knox's car that Madison will drive, I have no idea what just had happened. But in the rearview mirror, I see Knox stepping toward Drew.

21

DREW

Rubbing my jaw, I watch Madison and Lucy drive away.

"Did you hear what I said?" Knox repeats himself as he stands next to me.

My head turns to him, and I throw him a steely look.

"Lucy gets overwhelmed, just let Madison take her home," Knox explains.

I scoff a sound. "You really have no clue? She is a bit more than overwhelmed. She's been pushing along for years, and she might actually break."

Knox seems to still and take in my words, concern apparent in his face. His cheeks tighten and his hanging fists ball at his sides. "That may be, and I'll check on her later, but I believe she wanted us to talk."

Swiping a hand across my face, I'm not sure where to begin, as I'm fuming mad. "I don't fucking understand. Why would you not tell me about Hudson visiting?"

His shoulders go slack, and he leans against the brick. "I promised him."

"You don't even know him, but you do know me. Shouldn't I matter more?"

A smirk nearly forms on his mouth. "He's coming from a good place. Like I said, he was looking for Grayson. I guess he knew that you work and hang out with us. Maybe he was investigating us more than anything, double-checking that you're surrounded by honest people. He mentioned you two were getting to know one another, and his story checked out. Hell, I doubt Hudson Arrows would just show up with some far-out story, not to mention you two look alike. Anyway, the man seemed desperate to see that you have a good life."

"He lied to me." I cross my arms, completely let down.

"Trust me, this isn't the lie to get angry about. He's just being a dad, a *real* dad."

Shaking my head in disbelief, I refuse to believe it.

"Lucy's right, don't find a reason to push away someone."

"Because you haven't done that?" I give him knowing eyes.

It only makes Knox grin, because he is a confident fucker. "If you step back, then you might actually see that Hudson is the least of your issues right now."

Our sight on each other feels tense. "Oh, I know. You've made it clear that I'm not good enough for your sister."

Knox makes a ridiculous sound before half of his smile stretches on his face. "That's far from it."

"The other week you couldn't have been more clear about your thoughts on Lucy and me," I remind him.

He shakes his head. "Was I thrilled? No. Did I handle it well? Nope. Does it mean that I think you're not worthy of my sister? Hell no, I think you are exactly the kind of guy who will be waiting for her when we walk her down the aisle one day. But your timing to tell me the news? Fucking horrible."

"Would there ever be a day that is right to tell you that I'm together with your sister?"

"Yes. Not the day I find out that I'm going to be a father to two babies."

My eyes bug out at his news. "W-what?"

Knox sinks against the brick and lowers his body until he's sitting on the ground. "Madison is pregnant… with twins."

I can't control my smile. "And you found that out that day?" I follow him and also sit against the building.

"Five minutes before I found out my best friend is sleeping with my sister… yes!"

I rub my chin, trying to wrap my head around this conversation. He isn't angry at me; he's overwhelmed, just like Lucy. "Shit. Timing wasn't my forte on this then." I reach over to nudge his shoulder. "That's big news. You're going to be a dad."

"Nobody knows yet, still too early. Madison is probably telling Lucy now. But yes, my head was about to combust that day." He seems utterly defeated.

"And there I was making it worse."

He shrugs a shoulder. "Nah. I mean, yes, but I'm still able to talk to you. I'm more comfortable sharing this with you than my brothers who already have their families wrapped around their fingers. You've been my partner in crime, camaraderie without kids for a few years. Now everything is changing. You sure as hell can't talk to me about your dating life."

"Probably a good idea," I lament. But still, I'm slightly puzzled. "How come you've been a bit cold with me?"

"Digesting the news. Not going to lie, you're a great guy, but the image of you and Lucy is a bit… It takes time… and I don't want you two to put us in a position where I have to choose sides because that would suck."

"I see."

Silence takes over us as we both contemplate this conversation. I'm still torn about Hudson, but now better understand Knox.

"Lucy is special. I'm not blind to the fact that she has probably pushed herself too hard. But that's even more reason you need to have your shit together," he says bluntly.

Holding a hand up, I stop him from going further. "I know she deserves it all. A big house, a lavish wedding, and someone who can provide for her and give her nice things."

"She doesn't care about that stuff. All my sister needs is someone who will let her in, and you have. But the one thing that Lucy Blisswood is afraid of but will never admit is that she will lose one more person in her life who she loves. Don't give her any reason to believe there's a chance that you'll push her away." His tone is nearly stern.

My lips part open, as if a word wants to come out, but it doesn't. For a moment, I realize that Lucy has been watching me for weeks be a man who can't easily make a clear decision. With her, I was hesitant but kissed her anyway, then cautious until I agreed we should be together. Then she watched me with Hudson, and it's the same story, one step forward and another step back.

"I keep thinking that I can't have both, a father and Lucy. Why would the world be so good to me at the same time, you know?" I wonder aloud.

Knox brings his hands behind his head. "Maybe because fate decided that welcoming your father into your life involves Lucy. We all know only she has the power to get through to you. We've watched you two from the sidelines for years."

His theory crazily makes sense. "For years?"

He laughs at my face. "I struggled to get on board, doesn't mean I'm fucking blind. You two have looked at one another the way soulmates do, and I can say that shit because I have a great woman who is now my wife, so I know things."

I nod humorously. "You know things?"

"He pretends to know things." Grayson's voice breaks our scene, and we both look up to see Bennett and Grayson come out of Rooster Sin. They stand over us, and it causes Knox and me to rise from sitting until we're all standing in a circle.

"Everyone good?" Bennett surveys the group.

Looking at Knox, we both seem to have approval on our faces. He touches my arm briefly and answers his brother. "Now we are. I mean, we still need to have the boxing session we missed, where we both probably want to get out some aggression, but for now we're good."

"Even about Hudson?" Grayson isn't quite convinced of Knox's summary.

I bite my inner cheek. "I think my issue now is between Hudson and me."

Grayson steps forward to touch my shoulder. "Fathers do crazy things, and sometimes we go behind our kid's back. Doesn't always gain us points, but sometimes we have to, otherwise we'll go crazy. Hudson is just watching out for you, and so what, he did it wrong. Isn't the father thing new to him? Don't let it eat you up."

"Kind of hard to focus on that when I know Lucy is upset," I admit.

Bennett smiles faintly. "Putting our sister in front of your own emotional wounds. Nice."

Grayson gives Bennett the stink-eye, unimpressed with his casual tone.

"Listen, you'll figure it all out," Bennett says. "You have

to, otherwise, yeah, our work meetings are going to have a whole new fucking awkward dynamic." His tone is half-truthful and other parts playful.

Grayson indicates to Bennett that it's time to head to the car. "They will. I mean, we still need to have a big Blisswood wedding at Olive Owl, and since we all skipped that, then our money is on Lucy, she's the last resort." He winks at me before guiding Bennett away.

It leaves Knox and me alone once more. He seems fairly relaxed now and notices that I'm watching him as his eyes go wide. "Hey, I'm waiting for you. You're my ride since Lucy and Madison took my car."

I nod, and a smirk wants to form. "Thank fuck we reconciled then," I quip.

He laughs, and we both head toward my car. When we get in, he drags his seatbelt across his body and then gives me an inquisitive look.

"So, Hudson Arrows." He raises his brows. "Think you can get us box seats?" Knox says it in good jest, but barely, because he's serious.

"Too soon, buddy, too soon. You just made me sweat it out for a while that you would never be okay with Lucy and me. I'm not going to do you any favors," I inform him light-heartedly as I reverse the car.

Knox's signature smooth grin comes out. "Fair enough. But if that changes…"

Shaking my head, I ignore him. Instead, my mind wanders to Lucy and the fact that I need to see her, because I'll be damned if I'll let her be angry with me or even worse.

22

LUCY

Lying on my side on the bed, I feel like a rock.

Music plays softly in the room as I stare at the floor and debate if tonight is a break-open-the-wine kind of night, because truthfully, I'm not sure if I'm thinking clearly anyway.

Madison took me home, and the moment we entered the house, both Brooke and Madison were quick to usher me to bed, bring me tea, and suggested face masks, as if a girls' night would cure everything.

The moment they got the clue that Lucy may have gone a little loco for the night, they changed their demeanor to back rubs and silence, while I wallowed in a mood that I'm not quite sure I've experienced before.

They left me alone to sleep, but I don't want to sleep. I feel bad for snapping at Drew, even if it may have held a tiny morsel of merit.

I hear a gentle knock on my door, but I don't do anything about it—that would require energy.

The knock grows a little louder, and I huff a sound

because I know Grayson is due a check-in, and he won't relent until he confirms I'm okay. "Come in," I grumble.

Damaging blue eyes that make me even weaker meet my own when Drew steps into my room, with his dimples on display and a soft comforting smile.

Wiping my nest of hair to the side, I don't get a chance to sit up as he's already beside me on the bed with his hand on my hip before he even says, "Hey."

"Hi."

Drew looks around the room. "This is my first time in here with you."

"Surprised Grayson let you up. He's strict on his rules." I roll my eyes.

"I'll take the punishment." He begins to comb my hair with his fingers, trying to soothe me. "I'm worried."

"Fair point. I did go a little crazy, flip out, and possibly make you question your logic for being with me. Trainwreck? Yep, that would be me. Did I sum it up?" I offer in explanation.

He tries to hide his smirk, but I see the remnants of one on his mouth, his cheeks rough with a little end-of-day stubble. "And I'm the guy who is literally trying to ruin a good thing. Call us even?"

My lips quirk side to side. "I think I'm a mess."

"A beautiful mess," he counters.

Slowly I adjust my body and sit up in bed with a throw blanket bundled around my waist. "No, I mean, what if I made a mistake about quitting college, assuming I'd be some literary hotshot and not living in my brother's house."

He swipes a hand across his jaw. "I would say all of that is fixable. May need a little time, but it can all be remedied."

I hum at his answer. "I guess." I shrug. "What about you and Knox? I've screwed that up too."

Drew takes my hand in his. "Nah, you didn't. And your outburst at Rooster Sin kicked us into a conversation. That's all good now."

"Really?" I ask, skeptical.

He rolls his shoulder back. "I mean, family dinners may be awkward for a while, but that's more the image of us together that haunts him. Kind of funny if we think about it. And fuck, I'm screwed if I ever buy you the wrong birthday present because he will never let me forget it. But I think we'll be okay."

"And Hudson?"

He pauses, and his lips roll in as he thinks about my question, then he sighs. "A work in progress maybe. I think I understand why he did what he did, or why Knox felt the need not to tell me about Hudson's visit."

"A work in progress." Not promising, because we will continue to waltz back and forth on the one issue that scares me. "How do I know you won't one day wake up and feel like I'm not for you because you think you don't deserve someone in your life?"

He doesn't answer or seems stuck on his words.

"Drew, I can only be with you if you truly believe that I'm not going anywhere or that I won't let you down. Because right now, your conviction is a little shaky. I want to be here for you, like always, but I'm not sure I can handle a broken heart either. Not when I'm a hot mess. I can barely look at my laptop without a tear bursting out from the reminder of my failure."

Drew sweeps my other hand into his own then squeezes my palms. "You're anything but a failure. You are the glue for this family."

"Great, I'm goop," I quip, not impressed.

He chuckles softly. "Wrong word. I just mean, because of

you, everyone is happy. All of your brothers ended up with a wife because of you. Your nieces and nephews adore you. And I, well, I've been waiting for you my whole life."

My head perks up slightly. "Me?" I want to play it cool because his words wrap through every vein inside of me.

"Yeah, the kind of person who is going to kick me in my ass when I push people away who I probably shouldn't. The type of person who I need to kiss day and night, and I'm not quite sure why I haven't yet done it right now."

"Because I'm a pile of mush," I deadpan.

"But a fucking gorgeous pile of mush." He leans in and kisses the corner of my mouth once, twice, three times, before planting his lips on my own that must still taste like salty tears. He cradles my head in his hands to keep me in place, possibly in control.

"Lucy, I promise you I'm going to find a way to show you that I won't walk away."

I swallow my emotions because I'm feeling an array of them. "I don't want you to show me, I want you to believe in it for yourself."

He drags his thumb along my bottom lip. "Okay."

"Okay?"

"We both have work to do. You need to take it easy and truly assess what you want college-wise, then make a decision. You already know what we all think, but it's your decision. And me, well, I need to do a few things that involve people, my favorite thing," he jokes, and it makes me chortle a laugh.

I squint one eye as my fingers play with the blanket. "Do you think maybe we both should sort out our own lives before trying to be together?"

Drew seems taken aback by my suggestion. "I'm going to pretend I didn't hear that suggestion."

"What if it's true?" I'm serious, and I hate that.

"I'll prove to you otherwise." Now he just sounds confident. "Come here."

He pulls me against his chest into a big warm hug. Nobody would take Drew as a hugger, and he isn't, except with me. I inhale the scent of his shirt and wrap my arms tighter around him.

For a few minutes, he just holds me in his arms, and I can breathe again; I don't feel like life is suffocating around me.

"What the hell?" I hear confusion in his question.

Pulling back, my eyes draw a line from his to what he's looking at, and I laugh. A drawing that Rosie made for me of her horse, herself, and me. "It's the invite for Cosmo 2.0's birthday party."

"The horse is having a birthday party?" Drew's eyes widen from the absurdity of it.

I have to grin now. "I mean, a small one. Then again, you never know how much Rosie has wrapped Grayson around her finger. I think your invite is downstairs, with hearts on it. Mine, well…"

"It looks like Astro is eating your arm."

I lean against his shoulder and we both examine the drawing of Rosie on her horse, and me standing near the stallion who is biting my arm.

"He is. She's a little upset that I've taken him riding a few times, so I think it's the eight-year-old's way of saying back off her horse. Or it could be she's angry I stole her Prince Charming." I raise my eyebrows at him because she has a little crush on him.

Drew laughs at my explanation. "Family."

I nudge his arm. "Exactly. They do things that make no sense, but you love them anyway."

He absorbs my subtle hint; I can see it in his facial expressions.

"You should probably get some rest." He slides his knuckle along my cheek.

"Yeah," I breathe.

Drew showers me with kisses along my jaw to kiss me goodbye. When he slides off the bed and heads to the window, I look at him, puzzled. "What on earth are you doing?"

"Sneaking out."

"They know you're up here," I remind him humorously.

His head tilts to the side gently. "True. But maybe this is more fun."

I ruefully shake my head. "If you do that then they'll just assume that we had sex."

I love when he licks his lips. "A solid point."

Meeting him in the middle of the room, we step toward one another. "We'll figure it out."

"I hope so."

He gives me a gentle nod before he leaves out the door.

Sighing, I fall back onto the bed and look at the drawing, scoff a sound, and place it to the side.

Maybe I'm being ridiculous today about me and Drew. Or maybe I'm hopeful.

Either way, I won't get an answer tonight. Believing Drew will never let go is going to take a little more convincing.

DREW

I step to the side of my doorway to allow Hudson to enter my home. After seeing Lucy, I called him to inform him that I knew he had been to Olive Owl. To my surprise, I didn't go off the rails and instead asked him to come to Bluetop so we could talk.

Nonetheless, I can tell Hudson is nervous.

He tucks his sunglasses into his white t-shirt that accompanies his jeans. Jesus, he somehow looks even more youthful today.

"I'm relieved you invited me here," he begins.

I motion to the sofa to sit. "Truthfully, I'm amazed too."

He sits down, and his hands come up to stop me from speaking further. "I have some explaining to do."

I sit on the opposite lounge chair and fold my arms. "I would say so. Mostly, though, you seem smart, so you must have known that I would figure it out." Even I can't help but let a faint smirk form due to that fact.

Hudson sighs. "Maybe I don't mind, or I knew and was counting on it." It almost comes off as a challenge.

"I don't get it."

He gets comfortable and leans against the back of the couch as he angles his body in my direction. "I'm not afraid to say that I want to know every little thing about you. And I know you told me that you have a good life and not to worry, but... I couldn't let it go. I just had to know that you were telling me the truth, see it for my own eyes."

"So, you go to my place of work," I blankly counter.

A low chuckle gets stuck in his throat. "Not my best move, but when you mentioned work, not to mention my investigator who found you also brought up the Blisswoods a few times, then I couldn't wait to know that you're doing alright and not just telling me that to let me off the hook. Sure, I could have waited for the day you invite me into your life, but... I was going crazy waiting. You're my son." He swallows, and I see the sincerity in his face, concern and a form of emotion that I'm not used to seeing on a man unless it's Grayson or Bennett talking about their kids.

I tap my hands on my thighs in nervous habit, and I look around the room, but then I return to staring at Hudson sitting in my house. "Do you want a cup of coffee or something?"

The corners of his mouth curve up. "I'd love one."

I nod and get up. For the next few minutes, I busy myself in the kitchen, debating with myself, reminding myself, fucking giving myself the grace to go easy. Because pushing him away for an explanation like the one he gave seems like a shitty thing to do.

When I bring him a mug of coffee, I see that he's staring at my guitar. Handing him the mug, I decide to take the opportunity for a neutral topic. "I got it at a flea market of all places. Had to re-string it, but it's a good guitar."

"It has character. I like that." He takes a sip of his coffee.

A silence overpowers the room, and I realize that small talk just isn't going to cut it. "No more lies."

"No more," he echoes.

"This is my home, now you've seen it. Nothing fancy, but it's mine."

Hudson's eyes circle the room. "It's a nice place. I can tell you put in new dry wall and did a little cosmetic reparation; did you do that yourself?"

"I did." I set my drink on the coffee table. "Sounds crazy, but even if I had more money, I'm content with this place. I can build out if I want to expand, can sit on the porch on a warm summer night, and Bluetop is filled with good people."

"I get that. I would like to explore the town sometime if you don't throw me in your bad books." He sounds hopeful.

I scratch my head in contemplation of where to take this conversation. "Lucy thinks I don't let people in, and she thinks one day I'll wake up and push her away."

"Where is Lucy?"

"At her brother's, resting. She's, ugh, had a tough week."

"Oh, I hope she's okay."

Sinking into the chair, I think I'm about to give up. "She will be. Or at least I'm not going to be the reason she isn't having a good day. Calling you here was a selfish agenda because I thought if I make an effort with you then it may just prove to Lucy that I'm capable of letting people in. But the more I think about it… that's not what I want."

Hudson looks at me, confused. "Then what do you want?"

"I want you in my life because I want you in my life, not because I need to prove a point."

He slowly nods and seems patient to listen.

"I keep thinking that I'm used to being on my own. But the truth is that in the last few years, I haven't been alone at all. I have the Blisswoods, and when I told them about Lucy and me, I had it in my head that they would remind me that I'll never be their true family. In the end, it doesn't feel like that at all. Maybe I can be a bit more open than I thought," I admit for the first time.

"I can't pressure you, only support your philosophy."

I bite my lip and run through my thoughts to see if there's something else to get off my chest. I run a blank. "Do you maybe wanna go for a walk?" I throw my thumb over my shoulder. "It's probably dead in Bluetop, but Sally-Anne's has a good sandwich or Bear Brew has better coffee than my own."

Hudson sits up, clearly excited about my suggestion. "Lead the way."

―――――

WALKING ALONG MAIN STREET, we walk side by side. I point out all the spots on our journey.

"It's quiet here, but when it's the farmers' market, it gets insane, or when there's a high school home game. For some reason, lunchtime at Sally-Anne's is the place to be in a ten-mile radius," I explain.

"Quiet is good. I like staying on the down-low."

At that moment, Helen, who helps out at Olive Owl when she and her husband aren't in Florida, walks over to us. "Drew, yoo-hoo." She waves, overly excited.

"Hey, Helen, didn't know you were in Bluetop." I scratch my cheek.

"Of course, I'm a snowbird, so we still come back in the summer to see the grown kids. I even helped at Olive Owl the other week. What brings you to town with this strapping man… wait, I know you." She waves a finger at Hudson.

He looks at me awkwardly. "Ugh…" he croaks.

"I know. You were on that bachelor show." Helen seems confident with her answer.

Hudson grins because he has never been on said show. "I think you're mistaken."

She brings a hand to her chin to think. "Sports." She snaps her fingers. "You played for a baseball team."

"Nope."

I decide to throw her a clue. "Football, maybe."

Helen's face squinches. "Ugh, I hate the sport. Plus, Chicago's team had been playing really rotten lately."

I can't control the laugh that erupts from me.

Hudson clears his throat. "I would say they have room to make a comeback."

"Football is just a bunch of meatloaves on a field," she chides. Her attention returns to me with a smile plastered on her face. "Anyway, I hear you finally captured the heart of our young Lucy."

"If by young you mean a grown woman, then yes. Lucy and I are together."

Her hands come to her heart. "Always knew it would happen. Tell me in advance about the wedding so I can mark it in the calendar. Okay, need to run, take care." She pats my shoulder before she shimmies off, and her high-pitched voice says hello to her next victim.

Hudson looks at me, clearly entertained. "Wow, she's a character."

My brows raise. "You have no idea."

We begin to walk again, and Hudson nudges my shoulder. "Wedding?"

"Not there yet," I cut him off.

"Fair enough, but what's next for you and Lucy?" Now he's talking to me with a tone that is pure wonder.

I can't help but smile to myself. "I think, for now, she just needs to feel loved. Then one day she can move in with me and drive me crazy with her hair products everywhere, and one day I'll probably buy her a ring." Then when we're older, we'll have kids and I'll help coach the soccer team or something like that.

"Sounds like there's no probably about it, seems like a certainty."

Looking at Hudson, he grins with a knowing look, because he's right. It catches me off guard, partly because while the dream of a future with Lucy and I has always been in my head, I haven't shared it with anyone.

"For now, we'll focus on our beginning." Why does it suddenly feel like it's easy to talk to this man?

Hudson snorts a laugh. "Kid." He says that with a funny undertone because we both know it's ridiculous, considering our dynamic. "You're way past the beginning."

Yet again, he stops me in my tracks because there is truth in what he's saying.

I speak honestly. "It's been years of watching each other."

"Maybe it feels like the start because you're only just getting to the good stuff, right? Romantic gestures and I-love-yous. The stuff I hear grown men gush about, but I've kind of detoured it. But you, well, you function a bit differently to me."

Except I haven't yet said the most obvious thing to Lucy.

I smile faintly at Hudson in agreement. "You know, I think we can all agree that this meeting today has brought a bit of clarity, and the focus has been on me. But tell me more about the Arrows family."

"All right."

We make our way to Sally-Anne's, and after we order lunch, we sit down. Hudson has already explained that his parents, my grandparents, are retired. His mom was a teacher, and his dad was a manager at a plant, and Hudson has a sister.

Buying his parents a new car and house was the first thing he did when he went pro in football.

"And then there's April. Thought the uncle title would suffice. Why someone felt the need to make me a godfather, I'm not sure, but I couldn't say no. April is pretty easy with everyone, often comes to my games. I'm sure she would show you and Lucy around if you ever come to a game."

It dawns as me as I see people briefly landing their eyes on our table that I'm walking in public with Hudson, my dad.

I guess I had made a bigger deal in my head than I needed to, because this feels like a normal lunch. I'm not even tense like I was when we first met or even the second time.

Hudson continues to talk once the food arrives, but I don't hear a word. My brain is too loud with the message that if I take a chance, then this guy in front of me may just be like the Blisswoods who took a chance on me, and I let them into my life almost unguarded.

I've done this before, added people to my life. It turned out to be the best thing to happen.

Which is all the more reason that I interrupt Hudson when he's taking a sip of his drink. "This may sound kind of crazy, but what is your feeling on birthday parties for horses?"

24

LUCY

I walk into the kitchen because the sound of a mixer woke me up, which is fair enough, as it's pushing ten in the morning.

I'm groggy, but the moment I see Brooke and Madison busy with a mixing bowl then I'm awake. Not to mention a stream of natural sunlight is coming through the large windows.

"Hey there, sleepyhead," Brooke greets me.

Madison rubs my arm to welcome me to the scene.

"What the hell is this?" I ask when I see that there are already two levels of cake forming a tower.

Madison laughs because she finds this ridiculous too. "Someone requested a three-tier cake for Astro."

"He can't even eat it," I deadpan.

Brooke waves our notion away. "I know, I know, but it's all for fun, and why not, right?"

"I'm just here to lick the bowl of icing then help transfer the cake back to Olive Owl later," Madison says as she sits at the kitchen island.

Grabbing a spoon, I too take a little of the icing from the bowl to lick.

"How are you feeling today?" Madison asks.

I moan from the taste of the chocolate buttercream. "Okay, actually. The last few days of being lazy kind of gave me some perspective, you know."

"About school or Drew?" Brooke speaks into her mug of tea.

I smile to myself because they're probably as clueless as I am. I haven't seen Drew since he stopped by the other day, I just assumed he needed some space. For some reason, I'm not worried.

My family has been updated on my explanations of why I needed a break from life. They've been understanding. I did leave out the little details of my prior dating life. Occasionally, they ask to get a feel if I want to talk. Today being no exception.

"Let me have coffee first before we talk about this." I walk to the coffee machine and grab a mug. "Am I supposed to provide a present for this shindig later? I mean, surely a carrot for the horse will suffice?"

I grab my hair and pull it into a ponytail while I watch my coffee drip into a cup. I should probably change out of shorts and a tank top soon.

"Are you in a bad mood today? Because I'm picking up some vibes." Brooke gives me quizzical eyes as she holds up a spatula.

"I don't think she'll be in a bad mood for long." Madison flashes her eyebrows at me.

"Kind of hard to be when I'm surrounded by two pregnant people," I quip. Madison told me the news when she drove me home the other day and explained why Knox has been a bit more edgy than normal, and I couldn't be happier for them.

Grayson walks into the kitchen, and I wonder why he isn't at work. "Vacation day?"

He laughs sarcastically. "Funny. And you know we make our own schedules, and I wanted to be here."

"Be here for what? The realization that you have no spine when it comes to the demands of your eight-year-old daughter who thinks she's royalty?"

Madison and Brooke both stifle a laugh.

Grayson grins because I can tell even he finds it funny. "Or I'm here to see the look on my sister's face in about two minutes."

Immediately creases form on my forehead and I set my mug down. "What do you mean?"

"You don't have time, just check your reflection in the toaster or something." Madison makes a weird gesture with her hands.

Hesitantly, I look into the mirrored toaster to see that my messy ponytail is cute enough. No points for my lack of mascara.

"Why am I doing this?" I question.

"Drew made it out alive from his boxing session this morning with Knox?" Madison asks Grayson. "I saw them when I left."

Grayson grabs a bottled drink from the fridge. "I would hope so, considering he's outside and took time off work."

"Outside?" I gulp.

Before anyone can say anything else, the sound of a guitar outside hits my eardrums.

Brooke who was eating a spoon of cake mix drops it into the bowl. "Shut up, is that Drew?" She grins at her husband.

My brother shakes his head. "Yeah, he's trying to go all romantic on her."

I look to Madison. "Is this why you're here?"

She scoffs a sound. "No... uh... yeah. I'm not missing this."

A wide smile stretches on my face and I nearly skip to the patio door. The moment I'm outside, I see Drew near the pool under the pergola with one foot on a chair so he can balance his guitar.

My smile fades the moment I see a blue patch on his face. "Oh, shit." My hand covers my mouth. He stops playing instantly. "Did Knox really hit you during boxing?"

"Huh?" He touches the patch that my eyes are fixed on, then looks at his fingers. "Oh this, it's sidewalk chalk. Rosie was out on the driveway drawing. She must have got it on me when she hugged me."

"Phew." My hand finds my heart.

"Can I continue with my romantic gesture?" He grins.

I nod and stand there, unable to move as he plays his guitar and begins to croon.

Your smile may just make it worth the while,
Because honestly, I've been lost for too many miles.

I know I have an uncontrollable smile on my face as my hands come to my chest. He's playing a song for me.

But I felt it in my veins,
That one day something may change.

He plays more lines until he gets to a chorus, and then the sound of the last note lingers as the song finishes.

"Was that a Lucy song?" I ask, and I hear excitement in my voice.

Drew sets his guitar on the lounge chair. "It was one from the collection." He walks in a slow stride to me then tips his head to the side. "There may be a few more."

Now I know I'm smiling like a fool. My arms entwine around his neck before he kisses me on the cheek.

He takes my hands in his and walks us to another chair to sit on. "I think we should talk."

"Wow, thank God you didn't start this scene with that, because I would be deeply worried," I tell him. His jaw ticks which make me believe he appreciates my humor. I hold up one finger to inform him to wait a second, then glance back to the house to see an audience looking out the window. Gawking my eyes at them, they all disappear from the window. "Lack of privacy is sometimes a hazard in this family."

He tilts his head to the side. "You're right. I look for reasons to push people away, and the last few days I think I've come to realize that I don't need to, nor do I want to."

"Are you just saying that?" I have to pry.

He shakes his head. "No. I, uh, spent some time with Hudson. Invited him over, actually, and somewhere during the course of the afternoon, it just all kind of hit me like lightning."

"That's a big declaration."

Drew drags his finger up my arm and then moves to tap the tip of my nose. "It is. But I'm going to follow through on it." My face must give him a curious look. "I've already started texting with Hudson every day, and we have plans to meet again. Actually, you will see him later today, as I invited him to Astro's birthday."

I laugh at the utter absurdity of that sentence. "You invited your famous dad to a horse's birthday party?"

His grin is now wide, and his tongue draws a line along his lips. "I know. But what better way to move forward than invite him to a Blisswood family party?"

I grab his arms and guide them to wrap around me because I love his embrace. "That's quite a step. I mean, family meeting family and all, and a step you took for yourself, not us. I'm impressed."

"For some reason it feels natural."

"See what happens if you let go of your fears?" I give him a knowing look.

"Okay, Lucy, you made your point."

We get a little lost in one another's eyes as we sit there in a state of peace.

I swallow a breath. "I have also taken the last few days to think. It wasn't easy, but I decided that I'll transfer my credits to a place closer to home and then finish college."

He looks at me with piqued interest. "Is that want you want?"

"I think everyone *may* have a valid point that I'm so close to the finish line. But I don't think I can handle going back to New York. Madison helped me look into transferring my credits. Not all of them will transfer, but taking more time and being home is a good compromise," I explain.

Drew brushes his thumb against my cheek. "What about your writing?"

I shrug a shoulder. "I'll keep trying and maybe self-publish. I have time."

"Are you sure this is the plan you choose?" He seems doubtful, but more because he cares that I'm doing what's right for me.

"Yes," I promise.

"Good. So, it seems we're both on track."

"I guess so."

We both sit there with giddy looks and then something in Drew snaps. "Shit, I did this talk out of order."

"Did what out of order?"

"I was going to play you a song and then tell you I love you."

My head perks up in an instant. "You l-love me?" I stammer out.

He plays it cool. "Kind of obvious, no?"

I roll a shoulder back. "Maybe, but I like hearing it, especially since I love you too."

"I guess I'd better kiss you then." His rare suave look spreads on his face, right before he leans in and his lips plant on mine for a kiss that feels like a lightning strike to every molecule in my body.

It's a deep and longing kiss that steals my breath. When we pull away, I blink several times because I need to find my balance, even though we're sitting.

"This is turning into a great day," I confirm the obvious. "So, I have an idea to make it better." My finger plays with the edge of his short-sleeved shirt.

"Uh-oh, you want me to do something that would be wildly inappropriate right here."

"Not here, per se, but I do believe we have a window of opportunity between now and the party later." I wiggle my brows at him.

He surprises me when the palm of his hand lands on my ass. "Go get dressed, I'll be waiting in my car." His voice is a velvety breath that has me eager to change in a hurry.

———

LYING on the blanket in the back of his pickup, we stare up at the blue sky with a few white clouds floating by. We pulled over to a secluded spot in a field, and we have an hour before Hudson will arrive at Olive Owl.

"I wished for this. Every time you drove me in your car, I begged to the heavens that you would pull over and have your way with me." There is a whimsicality in my voice.

Drew moves to his side to look at me. "Maybe you were begging to the wrong place. What I plan to do to you would send me to hell."

My body wiggles against him, my dress skirt coming up to my waist. "Ooh, do tell me more."

His fingers trail up my thigh and sneak under my panties to slide along my wet folds. "For sure, we need to establish that these" —he pulls on the fabric— "under your dresses are kind of useless, nor are they a deterrent."

I feign shock. "Are you suggesting I show up to family functions ready to be fucked?"

His fingers pinch my clit gently. "No. I'm suggesting you save these for when you arrive to family functions. On the way over, you don't need them. Nor on the way back either."

I moan from the circle he is forming against my clit. "Uh, yeah, I can follow that rule."

"Good. Now touch me." His voice is a gravelly demand, and holy smokes, I love demanding-Drew. Such an opposite to the way he is with other people.

I slide my hand into his jeans and boxer briefs then take hold of his cock. "Wow, you're ready."

"Lucy, for you I'm always this way… and we're in a field and should be quick." He winks at me.

Without grace he pulls my panties to the side as I unzip his jeans. Moving slightly, he enters me from behind and he fills me up, making me feel full. His hand travels between my pussy and up to my breasts to play with.

"Deeper," I request.

He groans as he pumps into me, driving us to the edge.

"Tell me again," I whisper.

He stills for a second, his hand guiding my mouth into the direction of his own. "I love you."

"Lucky you, because I love you too."

He scoffs a sound before he returns to his mission to have me fall completely undone.

———

Parking at Olive Owl, Drew is ready to hop out of the car. Me? I quickly look in the rearview mirror to straighten my hair.

"Are you sure I don't look like we've just had sex?" I double-check.

Drew gives me an entertained look. "No. Now come on."

I blow out a breath and choose to trust his judgment.

We both close the car doors and look around, trying to figure out what direction the party is, considering Cosmo 2.0 is happily gnawing on some grass, alone in his pasture.

"Hudson is already here, I think," Drew mentions, and I love that he seems so at ease with this whole situation.

"Feed him to the wolves, geez. Didn't want him to wait for us?" I'm surprised, but then again, entertaining people is what my brothers are good at.

Right on cue, Hudson is walking out of the wine barn with Knox and Bennett by his side. They're all holding bottles of wine, which means they've given him a few to take home.

"Hey," Drew calls out.

Hudson looks up from his bottle and truly looks elated to be here.

That is until we all hear the blood-curdling sound of Rosie screaming. The kind of scream that immediately makes all our hearts sink. Quickly we run in the direction of the patio where she must be.

But as soon as we round the corner, we stop in our tracks and do our best to cover our laughs that want to erupt.

Because standing before us is Rosie in a summer dress, with sparkly sandals, a crown, and her hands in fists at her sides, clearly upset. Which is a fair emotion to have at her age, considering Pretzel, the giant dog, has two paws on the table and he's licking the cake nearly clean.

"Shit. Grayson's going to kill me, I thought I had Pretzel in the house." Knox is quick to grab the dog by the collar, but that cake is a goner.

"Welcome to our family," Bennett quips before walking to the cake to assess the damage.

Drew and I both look at Hudson. "I guess what Bennett said. Welcome." I smile and motion with my hands to the insanity around us.

25

EPILOGUE 1: DREW

I look at the barrels of wine as I sit there on a chair with my hands bound behind me. Shaking my head, I have to ask the obvious. "Is this really needed?"

"If you're going to ask us if you can propose, then you fucking better believe it." Knox leans against the wall with his arms crossed and a glint in his eye.

Grayson seems to be playing along with this interrogation. "Guys, let's go easy on him. He waited until Lucy graduated, and she pretty much lives at his house anyway," he says, recapping the past six months of my life since last summer when I finally plunged and took a chance on Lucy, on us.

"Where should we begin?" Bennett asks, and I still wonder why he's holding more rope.

I exhale loudly. "Yes, I'm going to propose. I came over to ask, but now I'm *really* questioning my traditional approach."

"Ring?" Knox asks.

"I went with Hudson, I picked one out when I was in

Chicago visiting him." Because Hudson is a part of my life now, football games and monthly lunches included. He even came out for the annual Blisswood holiday party.

"Simple but elegant?" Bennett double-checks.

"Yes," I reply.

Knox sighs. "How will you propose?"

I give him the death stare. "That's between me and her."

Bennett smiles at his brother. "This guy literally stood outside a window playing the guitar for Lucy. I think he has the romantic proposal down."

I do, I really do. In the back of my pickup truck, under the stars, with soft music in the background.

"Fair point," Knox agrees.

Grayson now is circling around me. "And the wedding will be here at Olive Owl?"

"I mean, I guess, if she wants."

All of the brothers now smile like they won.

"She has to say yes first," I remind us all.

They all laugh. "As if she wouldn't. I think she's already picked out a wedding dress." Bennett grins.

"Since you're all so confident about her answer, then again, why am I tied up?" I implore, only half entertained.

"This is more fun." Knox throws me a cheeky look.

Grayson holds up a finger. "You do know what marriage means, right? I mean, we don't need to have *that* conversation, do we?"

Blowing out another breath, I figure what the hell, and let's lay it all on the table. "A lifetime commitment. I'll take care of her, provide for her, I'll do whatever it takes to make her happy."

"Good answer." Bennett pretends to look at his nails.

These guys are ball busters, that's for sure.

"Bachelor party?" Knox claps his hands together.

My mouth gapes open because I can only imagine what's in his head. My shoulders go slack. "Hudson mentioned he wanted to arrange something, which is kind of weird considering he's my dad, but I guess he's more like a brother."

"Say no more. I'll take over the organization with him," Knox is quick to offer.

Now I have to cock a brow and grin, entertained. "If you're organizing my bachelor party then that means you agree that I can ask Lucy to marry me."

Now Bennett and Grayson laugh. "As if we would say no." Grayson shakes his head and smiles, then walks to me and unties my wrists. "It just didn't feel right to let you off easy."

Shaking my arms, the numbness slowly fades, and I feel the blood rushing back.

"I'm honored," I say sarcastically.

Bennett slaps a hand on my back. "This is going to be great. Olive Owl is going to have a Blisswood wedding at last. Our wine this year is really good, perfect for a wedding."

I give him an odd look. "You say that every year."

"True."

We all begin to walk out of the barn, but then stop when all three of the Blisswood brothers look at me.

"You've been part of the family for a few years. But it's even better now that you'll be official," Knox states.

And it's one of those times between men that you all acknowledge is a special moment, but you don't want to make a big deal.

Nonetheless, a round of awkward hugs it is.

And I feel lucky.

But I'll feel even more so when Lucy says yes.

That concludes The Blisswood Brothers. But what has Hudson gotten himself into? He kicks off the Lake Spark Series in book 1 of the new series coming in January 2023. Be sure to sign-up for the ARC! Yes...Drew will make an appearance :)

26

EPILOGUE 2: LUCY

Bennett looks at me and his eyes water, such a big softy. "Ready?" he asks as he offers me his arm.

"I think so. Your wife spent hours on my hair." I loop our arms together, and my veil is going to be my undoing because it gets in the way. Luckily my capped-sleeve lace dress is a normal length, and I'll even throw on Converse shoes later for the reception.

"You're my favorite sister," he tells me as we walk toward the back of Olive Owl.

I roll my eyes. "I'm your only sister."

"Still my favorite," he promises.

My heart begins to flutter when I see everyone sitting outside in rows. Everything is decorated like a dream. For years, Olive Owl has been voted as one of the most romantic places to get married; now I get to experience it firsthand.

"You didn't go overboard? I mean, just a little?" I hold my bouquet of flowers to the side and my hands indicate size.

He scoffs at my ridiculous notion. "It's not every day a Blisswood gets married."

"The mayor of Bluetop is here," I simply remind him.

"So is an entire NFL football team, it's all good."

He's also right. Hudson and Drew have become very close. Watching football is now a weekly occurrence in our house, whether on television or attending a home game. Hudson even took Drew shopping for his tux. He wanted to pay for the wedding, but my brothers would hear none of it. Instead, he gifted us a honeymoon.

"Ready for this, Lucy?" Bennett's emotional tone causes me to look at him, and I think I may cry.

"More than."

Everyone stands, and I suddenly feel all eyes on me as we arrive at the end of the aisle. Bennett leans in to give me a hug. "I'll see you again for that first dance." He nods to Grayson who takes over.

Having three brothers who have given so much time to watch over me is a logistical nightmare for weddings. But everyone has a part.

I see my nieces dropping flower petals from their baskets as the feeling of a new arm loops into my own.

"No turning back," Grayson jokes.

I look at him, almost bewildered. "I wouldn't even know how."

"That's good because he's a keeper."

We begin to walk down the aisle, and my eyes meet my future husband's. I've never seen him this dressed up, and it takes a moment to adjust to the view... not a bad image.

"Do you think this was how life was always going to be?" I ask my brother softly. "My wedding day like this?"

Cue the waterworks because I feel a tear stinging my eye, and I feel Grayson tense. "Lucy, you're going to kill me today... but yeah, our parents watching this up there are probably sipping wine and knowing that Knox, Bennett, and I ensured you ended up where you were meant the be."

"I think so too." I swallow.

Arriving at the front, I'm aware Knox isn't going to let any of us cry for long. The funniest thing about the running of Olive Owl? Knox was ordained a few years ago.

"I think we all know who gives away this lady. But Grayson, will you do the honors of confirming?" Knox already has a wicked grin.

"That would be her brothers." He leads my hand to Drew's then softly speaks. "Take care of her. She's something."

Drew clasps my hand with his. "I know, she's something beautiful."

Grayson shakes his other hand before taking a place as a groomsman next to Bennett who is now standing there.

"Hey there," Drew whispers.

"This is real," I say aloud.

"Very."

Knox clears his throat. "Shall we begin this thing? I have a timeline to follow, and if I mess up then I may end up in one of my sister's books."

Everyone laughs, and I give Knox a warning glare because I publish books now, and yes, my brothers may have influenced some of my fictional characters.

"Okay, let's make these two man and wife."

———

MY WEDDING RING shimmers under the fairy lights and mason jars with candles. Swaying in the arms of my husband, my fingers remain planted on his shoulders.

"Having a good day, *Wife*?" He pulls me tighter to his body.

"Have I stopped smiling?" I challenge him.

He twirls us around as a slow acoustic song plays. Everyone is having a good time as wine flows, and elegant tables are filled with food served family-style.

"How many times have you cried today?" I ask, curious.

His head jerks back slightly and he seems to be counting. "Twice. Hudson's pre-wedding talk which felt more like a team huddle and gameplan, yet he broke into pieces when he said he was happy to be here today. Then the other time was watching you walk to me."

I'm about to burst with a new round of tears. "I'm just a waterfall, a happy one, but at least you still seem on board, even though I have raccoon eyes."

"Totally on board."

We continue to dance, and I lean my head against Drew's chest, listening to his heart beating strong.

"Thank you," he whispers before placing a kiss on the top of my head.

"For what?"

"Being stubborn until I realized the chance I should take."

I laugh and pull gently back, which only makes his hands travel to my waist. "I'm stubborn? Nuh-uh. You're the king of that."

"True. Our kids will be screwed."

I swat his arm. "Good thing that ain't happening anytime soon." We have no need to hurry. I want to build up my income, Drew has taken on a lot of projects for Grayson, and we're young.

Getting comfortable in our dance again, I notice Hudson in the corner of my eye. "What's the deal with Hudson, by the way? He could have easily brought a plus-one, but he came alone."

Drew chuckles as if he has something fun to tell me. "That would be because he's seeing someone, but it's complicated."

"What do you mean? How do I not know this?" I look at him, completely surprised yet totally here for the latest gossip.

"She's young. Like, as in my age young."

"So? Not the first man to do that."

"Yeah, and she just so happens to be the best friend of his niece, and I'm not sure April knows yet."

My mouth shoots open and my eyes go wide. "This is awesome."

Drew chuckles. "I knew you would get a thrill from that."

"I want more details." I smile wide and am completely invested in this gossip.

"Not today. We have a reception to partake in before heading to our wedding night." He brings our joined hands to his heart.

I quirk my lips out. "We can go straight to the wedding suite upstairs."

Drew steps back instantly and laughs. "Hell no. I'm not skipping out on this party, the one your brothers arranged, the one that if we leave early then they will 100% never let me forget about it. I don't even want to know what the policy is on interrogating me now that their sister is legally married to me. I know there's a back room in the cellar that is always locked. Why do I have the feeling they won't be afraid to show me if I misstep?"

I shake my head, entertained, and grab his arms to pull him closer. "They're special, huh?"

"Sure." Drew throws on the theatrics of pretending to be

unconvinced. "Lucky me, I fell for their little sister, because the Blisswood brothers are exactly what we call one of a kind."

"Ah, so you agree," I tease him.

It earns me his arms wrapping around me so he can pull me into a messy yet delicious kiss.

THANK YOU

To anyone who reads this book, I hope you enjoyed the Blisswood family and their heartwarming family saga. Writing Lucy and Drew was bittersweet yet so worth it. I swoon every time that I think of them.

To Lindsay, another series and it wouldn't be complete without you.

Christopher, Peter, and Kate for making cover magic. Thank you.

Autumn at Wordsmith Publicity, where have you been? The missing puzzle piece. Thank you for helping spread the word.

Cheryl, thank you for taking on the not-so-fun tasks and making my life easier.

Bloggers, ARC team, grammers and tokers, I have so much gratitude for your help in sharing this story.

My other half, offspring, the damn cat staring at me, and my discovery of iced lattes...we survived another one!

Made in United States
North Haven, CT
18 October 2022

25634614R00127